THEN CAME MULVANE

Center Point
Large Print

Also by William Heuman and available from Center Point Large Print:

Heller from Texas
Guns at Broken Bow
On to Santa Fe

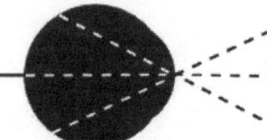

This Large Print Book carries the Seal of Approval of N.A.V.H.

THEN
CAME
MULVANE

WILLIAM HEUMAN

CENTER POINT LARGE PRINT
THORNDIKE, MAINE

This Center Point Large Print edition
is published in the year 2021 by arrangement with
Golden West Literary Agency.

Originally published in the US by Avon.

The text of this Large Print edition is unabridged.
In other aspects, this book may vary
from the original edition.
Printed in the United States of America
on permanent paper.
Set in 16-point Times New Roman type.

ISBN: 978-1-64358-917-6 (hardcover)
ISBN: 978-1-64358-921-3 (paperback)

The Library of Congress has cataloged this record under
Library of Congress Control Number: 2021930329

Chapter 1

A thin, misty, wind-blown rain swept across the open prairie as Mulvane moved past the muddy grove where the nester wagons were parked. His slicker buttoned tight around his neck, and his hat bent toward the rain, he let the big claybank gelding pick its way through the mudholes.

Here and there in the grove he could see bedraggled women trying to cook over smoldering fires. It was late afternoon and darkness was coming on quickly with the storm. Occasionally, a fire flared up, and Mulvane could see the light reflected on the soiled, rain-streaked canvas sides of a nearby wagon.

He felt some small measure of pity for these poor unfortunates exposed to the inclement weather, but the feeling was short-lived when he remembered other things, other times.

The claybank moved on slowly down the road toward the town of Rawdon less than a quarter of a mile away, and Mulvane kept his head toward the town, his jaw tight, the hardness in his gray eyes. He was a fairly tall man in the saddle, slim in the waist, deceptive power in the shoulders.

His hair was long at the neck, Indian black in color. There was a definite dent in his nose, and his chin had a deep cleft. It was a face which had seen much, and had been impressed by little; it was a face, too, which had things to remember.

Lanterns were lit in some of the wagons in the grove, and as Mulvane rode by the nearest one which was not more than a dozen feet off the muddy road, he saw someone open the flap and look out at him. Yellow lamplight revealed the face of an incredibly beautiful girl. It was a kind of wild beauty—the beauty to be found in a deep forest, or high up on a mountain trail.

Instinctively, Mulvane pulled up the claybank for a moment to turn his head and stare at the girl in the wagon. She had auburn hair, and her nose and mouth were perfectly shaped, the mouth full and rich.

The girl saw him, and she looked at him curiously, a faint smile playing around the corners of her mouth. She was neither shy, nor backward, and Mulvane was convinced that if he had pulled up to chat with her she would have been quite pleased.

He pushed the claybank on, however, the old dislike coming back to him stronger than ever. The sodbusters were all the same, man, woman, and child, although, perhaps, less tired and in a better mood, he would have made an exception to the girl in the wagon. They crawled out over the open rangeland like hordes of locusts consuming land which had been made safe for them by stronger, more courageous men.

They came uninvited, and they took what they wanted, the best water, the best locations, and they threw up their scraggly fences of barbed wire upon which the good range stock impaled themselves in the storms, leaving festering wounds and ultimate death.

It was more than this, though; it was more than the effect they had upon cattle. It was the devastation they brought to the souls of the strong men who had held these thousand hills for almost a generation before the first battered wagons arrived.

The sight of the nesters in the grove had reopened an old wound, even though he had known they would be in the vicinity of Rawdon, and he had come here expressly to deal with them.

The lights of Rawdon were straight ahead of him now as he rode down the little grade. It was not a big town, and Mulvane had seen a hundred like it during the past ten years moving from place to place.

Rawdon was strung out along the edge of a small creek. There were a few stores, a half dozen saloons, a fairly large hotel, and then at the far end of the town, the railroad station. He noticed a few drooping horses standing at the tie rails near some of the saloons, but for the most part the town seemed to be quite empty this weekday evening.

Riding up to the hotel, he turned down the alley to the stable at the rear where he dismounted and turned the claybank over to a wizened little hostler with a huge, bulbous nose standing in the open doorway.

"Good horse," the hostler nodded approvingly at the claybank.

Mulvane tossed him a coin, and then went on into the hotel to register. He wrote his name in a large, firm hand in the book, knowing that the clerk was watching him closely.

In a town like this, a stranger who rode in out of the rain was a rarity. Undoubtedly, strangers did come off the train, but there had been no train this hour. Mulvane had come up from the southeast, from a place called Wind Rock, his last job.

"Staying long, Mr. Mulvane?" the clerk asked.

He was a short man with a balding head and watery blue eyes.

Mulvane looked at him, a faint smile on his face. "Reckon you know how long I'll be staying," he said.

They knew he was coming, and undoubtedly the hotel clerk had been tipped off to watch for him. He was due in Rawdon on the eighteenth of the month, and this was the eighteenth. He was a punctual man. He was, also, an efficient one, as the Cattleman's Association of this county would shortly discover.

The clerk was looking at the register, a grin on his face, and he said, "An odd name, Mr. Mulvane."

Mulvane was not smiling now. He said, "Is it?"

The clerk blinked and rapidly changed the subject. He said, "Some of them are in town now, Mr. Mulvane."

"How many?" Mulvane asked.

The clerk thought. "Might be six or seven," he said.

"How many in the organization?" Mulvane asked him.

"Fourteen," the clerk said.

"They'll know where to find me," Mulvane said, and he picked up his key, slung his warbag over his shoulder, and went upstairs to his room. As he entered the hotel room on the second floor he could hear movement down below in the lobby, and he was quite sure that the clerk was sending a message to the ranchers in town that their man had arrived.

Closing the door behind him and locking it, Mulvane unbuckled his gunbelt and changed some of his wet clothing. As he was getting into a clean, warm, flannel shirt, he found himself thinking again about the nester girl who'd looked out at him from the wagon. She had wanted him

9

to stop and talk with her. She had not said it in so many words, but he'd seen it in the eyes of women before. He wondered if he would have pulled up if she had not been a nester.

A half-hour after Mulvane had entered the hotel room, he came downstairs and stepped into the hotel dining room, finding it nearly empty. After he had ordered his meal from the girl who waited on him, the hotel clerk stepped into the dining room, edged up to his table, and said in a low voice, "They want to meet with you in an hour at the lodge hall."

"Where would that be?" Mulvane asked.

"Little ways down the street," the clerk explained. "Second floor over the Alabama Bar."

Mulvane nodded. "Obliged," he said.

He saw the clerk's eyes slip down to the Colt on his hip, and then the man gulped as he moved away.

Mulvane ate a leisurely supper and smoked a cigar through before getting up from the chair. Looking out the window he noticed that the rain had stopped. More riders had come into town from the outlying ranches, and a group of nesters from the grove were coming down the street for a drink, obviously bored from sitting all this rainy day in the cramped wagons.

He watched them go by—heavy-footed, bearded men, accustomed to following the plow. One of the nesters was bigger than the others, a tall, raw-boned man with reddish hair and a red beard. This man Mulvane marked carefully. He liked to start with the big ones; by cutting them down to size he put fear in the little ones too. Before this night was over, the nesters in the grove would know about him.

As Mulvane watched, they angled across the road, entering the Cheyenne Saloon. Then a short, roly-poly man, wearing eastern shoes and a checkered jacket, crossed the road rapidly, following the nesters into the saloon. Over the bat-wing doors, Mulvane watched the nesters bellying up to the bar with the short, fat man squeezing in between two of them, slapping their shoulders as he did so.

Mulvane's thin lips curled in contempt as he watched the man, knowing him for what he was, an eastern land agent for this emigrant group which had moved in to usurp the land—land to which they may have had a legal right, but never a moral one.

He'd seen the type before—unscrupulous manipulators—who for a commission organized a group like this one, promising them excellent farm land and a thousand things which he never in this world could deliver. In due time the agent would collect his fee, and then run out, leaving the nesters with their grubby little patches of cultivated soil, which within a few years would become dust.

This land, Mulvane knew—as every other rancher knew—was grazing land. When you plowed up the soil you destroyed it as surely as if you dug salt into it. This the nesters would have to find out for themselves, and his mission in driving them out was almost a blessing in disguise. Not that he wanted to bless any of them.

As a child he had watched his father, old Whit Mulvane, die of a broken heart, his beautiful rangeland completely engulfed by these locust-like people who had squeezed him in, and eventually left him with nothing. Mulvane could never forget what they did to his father—a man who had fought the Kiowas and the Comanches for his land, and who deserved what he had as few men did.

Mulvane had his reasons, aside from the cold cash given to him by various Cattleman's Associations, for molesting the sodbusters wherever he found them. They didn't belong; they ruined the land, and he owed them one for old Whit, whom he had not seen since he'd doubled his age.

The Associations had heard of him in various places, and they were willing and anxious now to pay him the high dollar for his services. The nesters, too, in many cases knew about him. When he appeared on the scene, it was not unusual for many of them to pull up stakes and head for healthier climates.

Hiring a man like Mulvane had its advantages,

too, for the Cattleman's Associations, who as much as possible liked to keep their own hands clean. In Rawdon, however, Mulvane anticipated more than a little difficulty. There had been at least twenty nester wagons parked in that grove outside of town, ready to move out onto the rangeland. The challenge was there, and he was ready for it—one gun against all of them if the Association wanted to keep out of it altogether.

Getting up from the table, Mulvane paid his check and stepped into the street, moving down toward the Alabama Bar. An outside staircase led to the lodge hall on the second floor above the saloon, and as Mulvane approached the stairway from the south, another man came toward it from the opposite direction. He was a big man, heavier than Mulvane, his flat-crowned hat hung low on his head.

Mulvane slowed down, letting the other man go up the stairway first. He had a look at his face as the man went by. It was a hard, tough, square-cut face—the face of a man who was accustomed to having his own way and made no bones about it.

The man coming up the walk looked at Mulvane carefully, and nodded as he went up the steps. Mulvane had no doubt that he was one of the ranchers who were meeting here tonight with him.

He followed leisurely, noting when he got to the landing at the top of the stairs that the rancher ahead of him had left the door slightly ajar. He walked into the room, finding it smoke-filled even though only six men were in the place. It was an indication that they had been here for some time, waiting for him.

The room was big and barren, with chairs around the outer walls, and the ranchers were congregated in a corner at the far end. The big fellow who had just come in was standing alone near a window, touching a match to a cigar, and as Mulvane came into the room he was facing the door, and in the light of the three overhead lamps, Mulvane had a good look at his face. He had not mistaken the man. This fellow was a rough one, a tough jaw, pale blue eyes, ash-blond hair showing under the black, flat-crowned hat.

An older man, short, heavy-set with a paunch, and gray hair, got up from the chair in which he had been sitting, and walked down toward Mulvane. He said as he came up, "Mulvane?"

Mulvane nodded.

"Name's Harder," the short man said. "John Harder."

Mulvane shook hands with him briefly, nodding to the other men in the room who were introduced. The big fellow who had come up the stairway went by the name of Ward Bryant. His brand, as Mulvane remembered it, was called Rocking Chair.

Bryant made no attempt to come forward and

shake hands, but leaned against the wall, the lighted cigar in his mouth, arms folded, looking at Mulvane coolly out of those pale blue eyes. There was no friendliness in this man. Even though Mulvane did not expect friendliness from men who were hiring him to do their dirty work, he did not expect hostility, and he had the feeling that Ward Bryant was definitely hostile to him.

John Harder said, "Reckon that's all will be here tonight, Ward. Other boys all passed on this, already. We can get down to business."

Bryant said briefly, "Hannah's coming up."

Mulvane saw the faint surprise come into the gray eyes of John Harder, and the older man said, "Didn't know she was in town, Ward."

"Reckon she wanted to be in on this," Bryant told him. "Drove her in this afternoon. She's staying at the hotel, and should be up here in a minute or two."

Harder shrugged and looked at Mulvane, and then as if realizing that some kind of an explanation was needed, he said, "Hannah Carrington runs Box C up this way, Mulvane. She's a member of the Association. Box C is one of our big brands."

Mulvane shrugged, his gray eyes revealing nothing. It was the first time, however, that he'd had to deal with a woman member of one of these Associations, and he was not too sure that he was going to like it. He wondered, too, why this Hannah Carrington insisted upon attending a meeting such as this, which was primarily a man's affair.

Moving across the room, Mulvane sat down on one of the chairs along the wall. Pushing his hat back on his head, he rolled a cigarette, moistening the paper with the tip of his tongue, and then he touched a match to the cigarette.

There was no more talk in the room, but he had seen this happen before. Men who did not know him, or knew only of his reputation, lost their tongues when he was present. Yet Ward Bryant, who looked across at him brazenly through a haze of cigar smoke, made no attempt to conceal the dislike in his eyes.

Watching him, Mulvane realized that sooner or later, even though they were on the same side, he would have to cross with this man, and he wondered why.

Chapter 2

Mulvane had anticipated a middle-aged ranch woman, probably a widower who'd inherited her spread from her dead husband. He was scarcely prepared for the tall, slender, cool-eyed girl who came into the room. She was wearing a dress and a tan leather jacket, and she was hatless, brown-haired, blue-eyed, with a lift to her chin.

Mulvane had seen many thoroughbred horses, and he realized now that he was looking at a thoroughbred woman. He got up with the other men in the room, taking off his hat automatically.

John Harder looked at Mulvane, and then at Hannah Carrington. He said briefly, "Hannah— Miss Carrington, this is Mr. Mulvane, our man."

Hannah Carrington looked at Mulvane across the room, and then she nodded briefly, and he saw the contempt in her blue eyes. He tossed his half-smoked cigarette into a nearby spittoon, smiling thinly.

A tall, scrawny man who'd been introduced to Mulvane as Ad Baisley, said, "Reckon we'd better get started on this, John."

Harder nodded, and again he glanced at Ward Bryant, and Mulvane was beginning to understand the politics of this country. Bryant was head man around here, even if Harder apparently was president of the Association, and everybody knew it. Bryant said little, but he carried the big stick, and he was the tough one. He also seemed to be on the inside track as far as Hannah Carrington was concerned. He'd driven her into town this afternoon, and now as they sat down on the chairs in the corner of the lodge hall, Bryant sat next to Miss Carrington.

Harder said, "Reckon you know why we brought you here, Mulvane, and there's no difficulty about the price."

"No difficulty," Mulvane agreed.

He sat on the edge of the chair, leaning forward, elbows on his knees, his hat between his hands, moving it around with his fingers.

"There are about twenty nester families in that grove south of Rawdon," Harder explained. "Maybe you saw them on the way up, Mulvane."

Mulvane nodded.

"Man by the name of Arno Quill brought them here," Harder went on. "Damned easterner. Like to ride him the hell out on a rail."

Mulvane knew, now, who the fat man was whom he'd seen in the Cheyenne.

"This bunch," Harder added, "is all set to

18

spread out into the valleys around here, and we aim to discourage 'em a little."

Hannah Carrington said, "We don't want any killings, Mr. Mulvane."

Mulvane stopped twirling his hat, and looked across at her, his gray eyes fixed on her face, a faint smile almost of derision playing around the corners of his mouth.

"Reckon you'd like to start a little fire, ma'am," he observed, "but you don't want any one burned. That it?"

Hannah Carrington reddened slightly. "You're being well-paid," she said tersely. "I should think you would want to work with us."

"Work alone," Mulvane told her. "Reckon I don't need any help, ma'am."

Ward Bryant spoke for the first time since the meeting had begun. He looked steadily at Mulvane and said two words.

"Easy, mister."

Mulvane looked back at him, knowing that he had a man here who in another way was as hard as himself.

John Harder said hurriedly, "We figured with your reputation, Mulvane, there might not be too much trouble. Fellow down in White Springs told me you'd chased them off without even firing a shot."

Mulvane shrugged. "Might be different here," he observed.

"Why?" Ward Bryant demanded.

Mulvane smiled. "They might be tougher," he said softly.

Ad Baisley said glumly, "This crowd gets out o' that grove an' on to our ranges, an' there'll be a hundred more of 'em next month, an' five hundred afore the year is out. We got to stop 'em now."

"With guns?" Mulvane asked him, "or with talk?"

Baisley looked at him, and then down at the floor, and he had no answer.

John Harder said, "We're asking you to help us clear these damned nesters out, Mulvane. Reckon it ain't up to us to tell you how to do it. We don't figure on you, though, ridin' up and down these ranges, and shooting people down. We got some law in this town."

Mulvane smiled at him. "Who owns the law?" he asked.

He'd known from past experiences that an Association like this would never bring a man like himself into a territory unless they owned the local sheriff, lock, stock and barrel, and tin star, also.

Ward Bryant said, "You want the job, mister?"

Mulvane looked across at him. "You wanted me," he observed. "I rode two hundred miles to get here. You figure I ought to turn around and go back now?"

John Harder said quickly, "Ward, we made a deal with this man, and we'll have to stand by it."

Mulvane stood up. "Anything else I ought to know?" he asked.

He saw Hannah Carrington staring at him as she sat next to Bryant.

"We figure," Harder told him, "that this Quill fellow will start moving the nesters into the hills any day now. He's been trying to clear things through with the local land agent. The first wagon leaves that grove has to be stopped. Reckon we know that, Mulvane."

Mulvane nodded. As always the first leak in the barrel was the worst. If they plugged that up they could stop the others.

Harder took a check from his shirt pocket. "Here's five hundred now," he said, "and you get the other thousand when we're satisfied that this bunch is on the move and won't come back."

Mulvane put the check in his pocket, and then put on his hat and headed toward the door. Harder said, "If you need any of our boys, Mulvane, just let us know."

"We'll see," Mulvane answered.

He was at the door when he heard the light step behind him, and turning around he saw that Hannah Carrington had followed him. He looked down at her, noting that Ward Bryant was watching them carefully from the other end of the room.

Miss Carrington said, "I want to repeat what I said before, Mr. Mulvane. I would not like to see any of these people killed."

"They'll be asked to move on," Mulvane told her. "The first wagon moving out of that grove will be told to go back."

"What if they don't?"

Mulvane shrugged. "We can hope they do," he said.

He saw Ward Bryant coming up behind her now, and he knew that Bryant didn't like Hannah Carrington speaking with him. As Mulvane turned to go, Bryant called to him, "Hold it up, Mulvane."

Mulvane waited. Hannah Carrington walked away, knowing that the two men probably wanted to talk alone.

Bryant said as he came up, "One thing you have to remember up this way, Mulvane."

"What's that?"

"When you deal with us," Bryant snapped, "you're not dealing with nesters."

"You came down here to tell me that?" Mulvane grinned.

"You're hearing it," Ward Bryant said tersely, "and remember it."

"I'll remember nothing," Mulvane told him, and he turned and went down the stairs to the street.

It was about eight o'clock in the evening. The

22

rain had completely stopped, and a sliver of moon was sliding out from behind a dense bank of clouds as Mulvane moved down the street, heading toward the Cheyenne Saloon.

In his shirt pocket he had the five-hundred-dollar check from the Cattleman's Association. He had a job to do, and tonight was as good a night as any to get started.

When he entered the Cheyenne he saw the nesters still at the bar—five of them including the red-haired fellow with the beard. Arno Quill, the land agent, was now sitting in at a card game at one of the tables. He had a round, greasy face with deep-set, amber colored eyes and straight black hair. There was very little neck to him, his round head sitting upon his shoulders like a pumpkin on a fence.

Mulvane moved up to the bar, taking his place next to the red-bearded fellow. He stood there, elbows on the wood, hands clasped in front of him, a cold smile on his face as he looked into the bar mirror.

When the bartender moved over toward him, he pointed to a bottle on the shelf, and then placed a coin face down on the bar wood. He had his drink, and he listened to the nesters talk. They sounded like midwesterners to him, Indiana men possibly, with a twang to their speech, and the soil in their talk.

These men knew nothing of the open range, or

23

of cattle, or of winter storms which hit this part of the country with terrific fury. They knew nothing as yet of the heat, the monotony, the loneliness of life on the open plains, and they'd been talked into coming out here by a smooth-talking agent.

Looking over at Arno Quill, Mulvane had the feeling that he would like to step up to the small man and smash him full in the face, squashing it like a pumpkin.

The red-haired nester turned his head slightly to look at the man drinking next to him, and Mulvane said aloud, "Take a good look, mister." He said it loudly enough so that the other nesters could hear it, and immediately silence fell upon the rest of them. They had heard the definite hint of trouble in his voice and sensed that he was going to prod them.

The red-haired man didn't want any trouble either. There was anger in his eyes, but he turned away.

"Sodbusters," Mulvane sneered.

He turned around, placing his elbows on the bar wood, and stood there, facing the room, looking around. He noticed that Arno Quill had looked up when he had spoken, and the fat man had now put his cards, face down on the table, and was staring at him, a frown on his chubby face.

"Who's the boss of this outfit?" Mulvane asked, "Or do you all run like sheep?"

The red-haired man said gruffly, "We got no quarrel with you, mister."

"Sodbusters," Mulvane repeated. "Cow milkers."

There was a taunt and a challenge in his voice now, and he waited for someone to pick it up, knowing that they wouldn't, and that he would probably have to push this thing a little farther before they did.

Arno Quill got up from his chair at the card table, and moved toward the bar—a little buff rooster, his flabby hands in his pockets, a stub of cigar in his mouth, and his brown derby pushed back on his round head.

He smiled placatingly and said, "Cowboy, we don't want any trouble with you."

Mulvane said to him, "You bring this crowd here, mister?"

Quill nodded and smiled. "I represent the Indiana Emigration Company, and I am responsible for these men."

Mulvane looked at him, watching the stub of cigar wobble in his mouth as he spoke. He didn't like the sight of it. Without a word he lashed out with his right hand, slapping the cigar from Quill's mouth.

The fat man's face went white, and he stepped back a little. Then he smiled and opened his coat. "I'm not armed," he said. "You can't pick a fight with me, mister."

Mulvane just smiled at him, and then raised his boot, placed it against Quill's stomach, and pushed hard. The fat man tumbled back against the card table at which he'd been sitting, upsetting the table, cards, glasses, and a bottle, and then he went over the top of the table, landing on the floor on the other side.

He was not hurt because Mulvane had pushed him with his foot, and he got up immediately, quivering with anger. Mulvane waited for someone else to pick it up, but the nesters at the bar hesitated even though there were five of them, and he was alone.

The red-haired farmer finally said, "Hadn't ought to have done that, mister."

Mulvane turned to look at him, remembering that this was his man. He needed a big man; pushing little Quill around meant nothing.

"What is it you want?" Mulvane asked him.

"Hell," the farmer growled. "Reckon you're the one came in here with the chip on his shoulder."

"Come and knock it off," Mulvane invited.

The nester scowled, but he'd stepped into the water, and there was no backing out now. He said slowly, "Take off that gun if you want any trouble, mister."

Mulvane unbuckled the gunbelt and dropped it to the floor. He had his moment of respect for the big farmer who had stepped out of the crowd to

26

face him. He was smiling as he said, "Come and get it, sodbuster."

The nester lunged at him, and Mulvane stepped in fast, smashing him in the stomach with his left fist. As the farmer bent over double, gasping for air, his face turning a greenish color, Mulvane chopped him on the side of the face with his right fist, and then slashed down hard again with the left, dropping the nester to the floor.

When the nester started to climb to his feet, Mulvane slammed him hard again with his left fist, propping him up against the bar, and then tore in with both fists to the body, almost ripping out the farmer's middle.

The nester slid down the bar. Mulvane continued hitting him until he was on the floor unconscious, bleeding from a half dozen cuts.

Stepping back and breathing hard, Mulvane picked up the gunbelt and strapped it around his waist. He looked at the nesters at the bar, who were staring down at the beaten man, dull-eyed, and he said, "The name's Mulvane. Remember that. You'll be seeing me around, and the first one trying to pull a wagon out of that grove will be seeing me sooner than the rest."

He went out into the night, then, and when the cool night air hit him he was a little sick the way he always was after an affair like this. He tried to tell himself that these nesters had come out here knowing that they would be running into trouble, that they were trying to invade rangeland, and now they had to face the consequences.

Walking back to the hotel, Mulvane stopped in at the stable to have a look at the claybank. He stood in the stall a few moments, rubbing the animal's nose, thinking of the job ahead of him, of Hannah Carrington and Ward Bryant. Then quite suddenly he found himself remembering the nester girl he'd seen in the wagon riding in early this evening.

He'd made a start in this fight against the nesters; he'd put the fear into them, and they knew about him. How bad this became was now their own affair. If they wanted real trouble—gun trouble—he was ready for that, too, but he hoped it would not go that far, maybe for the sake of the girl in the wagon, and maybe for his own sake. He wondered if in years to come he would turn into a cold-blooded killer who had forgotten the reasons which prompted him to war on the nesters. Would he be killing only for the sake of killing?

Standing in the stall beside the claybank gelding, a cold sweat broke out on his face. Maybe he had already made that change, and he was not fully aware of it. Had Hannah Carrington seen that in his eyes?

Chapter 3

When Mulvane came down for breakfast in the morning he found the law of Rawdon sitting in a wicker chair on the porch. He was a fattish man, with a drooping, black mustache, and amber colored eyes. He wore a star on his vest, and a gun on his hip, but neither of these things meant anything.

The sheriff of Rawdon leaned back in his chair. He hooked a pair of flabby hands in his gunbelt, and he said easily, "New man in town?"

"You know me," Mulvane said, and he made no effort to keep the contempt out of his voice.

The lawman stood up. "Name's Ed Bagley," he said. "Hear you had a little run-in last night with one of those damned nesters."

"You heard right," Mulvane told him.

"Had to take that big fellow back to the grove in a wagon," Bagley grinned. "Reckon you worked him over pretty hard."

"You aim to lock me up?" Mulvane asked.

Bagley grinned. "That was no crime," he said. "Reckon that was a good deed, Mulvane."

Mulvane just looked at him, and then walked away. He didn't like the man; he didn't like Ward

Bryant, either, but he was committed to working with these men until this job was finished.

Going around to the stable, he saddled the claybank and rode south out of town. The day was clear and cool after the rain of the previous night, and the puddles in the road were drying up rapidly. Before the day was over, he knew that every drop of water which had fallen would have disappeared.

This was a dry and a thirsty land where the rain fell much too infrequently for the cultivation of crops. The tough buffalo grass survived on this kind of fare, but corn and grain and other crops would shrivel up and die when the heat hit them.

When he neared the grove he saw smoke ascending from a number of cook fires, and as he skirted the grove he noted that some of the nesters came out to the edge of the woods to watch him ride by. He knew that they recognized him.

They watched silently as he turned up the little creek which passed through the grove. This morning he was out to see this country, and to let the nesters know that he was in the vicinity. They knew him now; they knew of his reputation, and he wondered if any of them would attempt to leave the grove.

If they were all to leave at the same time, scattering out over the different ranges, they would of course give him more difficulty, but then, too, they would be separated, and he could handle them one by one. Undoubtedly, they knew this. He often wondered why some of them didn't band together to run him down, but then these farmers were not killers. They had come here to dig the soil, and violence was alien to them. They'd never fought the wild tribes to hold what was theirs, or battled the storms and droughts.

He rode up the creek about a quarter of a mile, and as he was crossing it—intending to ride up the grade on the opposite side—he saw a girl coming down creek with a berry pail. He had noticed many chokeberry bushes along the creek.

Mulvane had the claybank on the opposite shore of the creek when he recognized the girl as the one he'd seen in the wagon the night before. There was no mistaking her, the auburn hair catching the rays of the morning sun, the beautiful oval face, and then as she came closer, the friendly dark brown eyes.

She was wearing a cheap gingham dress, and her shoes were much the worse for wear for coming up here along the creek, pushing through the berry patches.

When she saw Mulvane, a quick, warm smile came to her face. He waited for her, not quite sure why. The girl walked up to where he was sitting astride the claybank, and she looked at the animal critically, then she said:

"You passed by our wagon last night."

Mulvane nodded.

"You have a beautiful horse," she said.

"A good animal," Mulvane agreed. He was puzzled by this girl. She was not afraid of him, even though he was a total stranger and they were far out of sight and hearing of the grove.

"I'm Ruby Watkins," she said. "Why didn't you stop last night?"

"Due in town," Mulvane told her gruffly.

He could see that she was several years younger than Hannah Carrington, and the vitality of youth was still in her.

"Why did you want to talk with me?" he asked.

Ruby Watkins shrugged. "It's lonesome in that grove," she told him calmly. "There are no young men. Every one is married."

"You come out with your parents?" he asked.

"An uncle," Ruby said. "My parents died back in Indiana years ago." She looked at him, a twinkle in her eyes, and she said, "You didn't tell me your name, mister."

Mulvane moistened his lips, and then bent down to rub the neck of the claybank, "Mulvane."

He knew that she was staring at him now, and she said slowly, "You're the man whipped Adam Leroy in town last night."

"Had a little trouble last night," Mulvane admitted.

Ruby was looking up at him, standing close

32

beside the horse, the pail of berries still in her hand.

"Why do you want to drive us out, Mr. Mulvane?" she asked.

"I don't like nesters," he told her. "They don't belong in this country."

"The country's big," Ruby smiled, looking around. "Surely there must be plenty of room for everyone."

Mulvane looked down at her, the knowledge in him that if he so desired he could bend down and lift her up to the saddle and kiss her, and she would not object. He had a strange compulsion to do so, but he fought it down. She was a nester like all the rest of them, and they had brought much misery to himself, and his family. Let alone, they'd bring grief here, to others and to themselves. Besides, he had a job to do.

"This is not farm country," Mulvane stated. "Your people will starve within a year or so, and you'll wish you hadn't come here."

"Is it true?" she asked curiously. "Are the ranchers in this area paying you to drive us out?"

Mulvane looked up the creek. "You ask a lot of questions," he said.

"I'd like to know about you," Ruby smiled. "You don't look as hard or as tough as the men in our camp say you are. Have you ever killed anyone?"

Mulvane scowled. She was like a small girl

prodding him. She said when he didn't answer, "I guess even though I know you and know your name you couldn't come and see me because you don't like us."

"I wouldn't be welcome in that grove," Mulvane half-smiled. "You know that."

"Would you like to see me?" Ruby persisted.

Again he had the feeling that he was speaking to a very small and lonely girl.

"Must be plenty of young men in town," he said.

"I've only been in to town once," Ruby told him, "and I haven't seen anyone."

"Keep looking," Mulvane advised. He knew that the young men around here would be flocking to her sod shanty like flies once they had a good look at her. As for himself he knew that he had better keep clear of this innocent girl with the brown eyes.

He was about to turn the claybank around and start up the grade when he saw two riders moving up over the top of the grade and coming down toward them. He recognized Hannah Carrington immediately, astride a black mare with two white feet, riding slightly ahead of a man.

The man was Ward Bryant on a big bay animal. Mulvane saw the surprise in Miss Carrington's eyes as she came down toward them. It was very evident that she had not thought that he was a ladies' man.

Ward Bryant's pale blue eyes were openly derisive as he approached. Mulvane cursed himself, and wondered how he could have been so careless as not to have heard their horses coming up the grade.

Bryant said caustically as he approached, "Working for us now, Mulvane, or for the nesters?"

"What does that mean?" Mulvane snapped.

"Make what you want out of it," Bryant told him thinly, and Hannah Carrington said quickly, "Please, Ward, let's not have any trouble."

"We're paying this man big money," Bryant said. "We're not paying him to be sparking the nester girls away from their camp."

Mulvane slipped one boot out of a stirrup, and then Hannah said, "Please come, Ward."

The two of them rode on, and Mulvane sat watching them, his mouth tight.

Ruby Watkins said, "She's very beautiful."

There was no envy in her voice, and she stared after Hannah Carrington admiringly. "Who is she?" she asked.

"Ranch woman in these parts," he told her. "Runs Box C."

"She owns cattle," Ruby said wistfully. "I don't own anything, not anything at all."

Mulvane put his boot back into the stirrup. "Reckon I'll ride on," he said, and he touched his hat to her.

He knew she was watching him as he rode the claybank up the ridge. He was annoyed with himself at having had Miss Carrington and Bryant find him with this girl, and the rest of the morning as he rode across some of the nearby ranges he was in a bad mood.

He passed plenty of cattle out in the hills, Box C, Rocking Chair, which apparently adjoined Box C, along with a number of other brands. As he rode across the range, which he took to be Ward Bryant's, he spotted two riders moving a bunch of cattle east in the direction of one of the ranchhouses. One of the riders moved away from the cattle and headed toward him, having seen him crossing a ridge.

Mulvane pulled up and waited, thinking, perhaps, this could be one of the ranchers he'd met in the lodge hall the previous night. The rider was on a dapple-gray animal, and he wore a worn, tan leather vest. He was short, heavy-set with reddish hair showing under the brim of his hat. His face was hard and tough, with a bulldog jaw.

The rider came up easily, pulling up the dapple gray a few yards from where Mulvane sat astride the claybank. He looked at Mulvane coolly.

"Mulvane?" he said.

"That's it," Mulvane nodded.

"Told me you were riding a claybank," the squat man said. "Name's Faraday. Jud Faraday. I ramrod for Ward Bryant."

Mulvane nodded.

"Any of them damned nester wagons leave that grove, yet?" Faraday asked.

"I'll watch for them," Mulvane said.

Faraday looked at him. "Like to play a lone hand," he grinned.

Mulvane shrugged. "Reckon I'm paid for this job," he observed.

Jud Faraday nodded to Mulvane giving him a grim, cold smile, and then he turned the dapple gray around and rode back to the bunch of cattle he'd been driving.

It was past noon now, and Mulvane headed back toward Rawdon. Moving past the grove again, he counted the number of wagons. There were nineteen, exactly as many as he'd counted that morning.

As he entered Rawdon, he saw Hannah Carrington coming out of the stable where she'd left her horse. When she saw him she waited on the hotel porch until he rode up, and seeing that she wanted to talk to him Mulvane moved over to the tie rail, dismounted, and tied the claybank to the rack.

He went up on the porch, touching his hat to her, and she said to him with a faint smile, "We seem to be meeting each other in many places, Mr. Mulvane. I want to assure you that we were not spying on you up along Ash Creek."

"And I wasn't hiding anything," Mulvane

said stiffly. "I ran across that girl as she was out berrying, and we got to talking. That's all there was to it."

Hannah Carrington nodded. Watching her, Mulvane made a mental comparison between her and Ruby Watkins. Ruby was a wild flower, beautiful, delicate, growing in the wilderness. Hannah Carrington was a marble statue, every detail perfect, turned out by a master craftsman.

She was watching him carefully, and she said now, "I do hope there'll be no trouble between you and Mr. Bryant. It would be very foolish of you to be fighting each other when you have a common enemy."

"Didn't come here to fight ranchers," Mulvane reminded her. "Your Mr. Bryant, though, has been getting in my hair."

Hannah smiled a little. "Why do you call him *my* Mr. Bryant?"

He shrugged. "Figured you knew each other pretty well," he said.

"We've known each other since we were children," Hannah told him. "We grew up on adjoining ranches. I guess Ward was the first boy friend I ever had."

"And the last?" Mulvane asked her.

Hannah looked at him steadily. "We are not engaged," she said, "if that's what you mean."

Mulvane wondered why not. They were of

38

marrying age. He figured Ward Bryant to be at least twenty-seven or -eight, and Hannah Carrington could be perhaps twenty-three, almost past marrying age.

"As a matter of fact Ward's been away for a number of years," Hannah explained. "He came back to Rocking Chair less than six months ago, after his father passed away. They'd had a little trouble when Ward was younger, and he'd decided to pull out."

Mulvane nodded, knowing now where Ward Bryant had acquired that toughness. Bryant had not been a peaceful rancher all of his life. He'd moved around a bit as had Mulvane. He probably knew how to handle a six-gun and his fists as well, and he took nothing from any man.

"Where's Bryant now?" Mulvane asked her.

"He rode back to the ranch," Hannah explained. "I'm staying in town another day. I have a shipment going out in the morning, and I'm expecting a cattle buyer on the afternoon train."

"You're staying at the hotel?" he asked.

She nodded. "I notice you're registered here, too," she said. She added, "I have my meals in the dining room."

Mulvane looked at her for a moment, knowing full well what she was driving at, and then he said, "Reckon I could see you for supper tonight?"

"That would be a pleasure," Hannah smiled.

Mulvane wondered if anything had happened between her and Ward Bryant which accounted for this sudden friendliness on her part. Last night she'd been almost openly hostile to him. Perhaps, seeing him with another woman had accounted for the change in her. Mulvane could only conjecture. It was impossible to know what was going on in a woman's mind.

As they stood on the porch a rider came into town moving very fast, heading straight for the hotel. Mulvane turned around, instinctively knowing that the rider had a message for him.

He noticed the brand on the man's horse as he dismounted at the tie rack in front of the hotel. It was Box C, Hannah's brand.

"What is it, Joe?" Hannah asked.

The rider said tersely, "Nester wagon just rolled out of that grove, Mulvane, headin' west. Figured you'd like to know."

"One wagon?" Mulvane asked him.

"Just one," Joe said laconically, and Mulvane knew that it was a test. The nesters probably wanted to see how far he would go in turning them back. He had no choice but to show them. He had given the nesters notice; he had thrown down the gauntlet, and they'd picked it up. The next step was up to him.

Without a word he went down the hotel steps, lifted himself into the saddle, and rode out of town. As he was passing the sheriff's office he saw Sheriff Ed Bagley come out, yawning as if he'd just finished a nap.

Bagley waved to him, but Mulvane kept going, not even acknowledging the greeting. In a few minutes he had reached the grove and was swinging around toward the west, taking up the trail of the lone wagon which had pulled away from the camp.

The nesters had seen him coming, and they were watching now as he skirted the grove, the claybank moving at a fast rate. They watched silently, sullenly, making no attempt to stop him as he took off after the slowly moving wagon less than a half-mile away.

He wondered which one of the nesters had the nerve to test him, and then even before he reached the rattling, dilapidated prairie schooner, he thought he knew.

A pair of broken-down mules hauled the wagon, taking their time about it. Coming up on the rear of the wagon, Mulvane saw Ruby Watkins looking out at him from the opening. She smiled warmly at him as he rode by.

The man driving the wagon was lean and thin, with carroty hair, and weak blue eyes. A drab woman sat beside him on the seat, seemingly uninterested in what was going on.

Mulvane said quietly, "Pull it up, mister."

He moved up to the mule on the near side, and

grasping the bridle, turned the wagon off the trace.

The man on the seat said dully, "Ain't no cause to stop us, mister."

"Where you heading?" Mulvane asked.

"Filin' a claim up along Ash Creek," the nester said.

"Not today," Mulvane told him, "and not tomorrow. Turn it back, mister."

Ruby Watkins had moved up to the front of the wagon now, and she was looking out between the two people on the seat. She said to Mulvane:

"Mr. Mulvane, this is my uncle Joab, and my aunt. They'll just be taking a very small piece of land."

Mulvane shook his head. "Turn it back," he said.

"This is a free country," Joab Watkins blustered.

Mulvane still held the bridle of one of the mules. He drew his gun now, and held it against the head of the mule.

"If I shoot these two mules down," he observed, "you'll have to pull this wagon, yourself. What will it be, Watkins?"

Ruby said, puzzled, "I thought because we were friends you'd let us go through, Mr. Mulvane."

"Can't let anybody go through," Mulvane told her.

He was looking at Joab Watkins, the gun in his hand, the muzzle against the head of the mule.

42

"Reckon I'll turn her around," Watkins said sullenly.

The woman beside him said nothing. She was dull-eyed and worn out from overwork, and apparently it mattered not to her whether they stayed in the grove, or filed a claim up Ash Creek.

Mulvane pulled the claybank back and let Watkins turn the wagon around so that it was heading back toward the grove. Joab said sourly, "You damned ranchers think you own the whole world."

"This little part of it," Mulvane told him. "Go back and tell your friends to head back home again."

"Land's worn out back home," Joab Watkins scowled. "Why in hell you think we came out here?"

"Try it some place else," Mulvane advised. "This door's closed."

Ruby was watching him, a slight frown on her face, but she was not really angry. She had undoubtedly told her uncle that she'd met the hired gun for the Cattleman's Association, and was on friendly terms with him, and Joab had assumed this friendship would give him a free pass on to the Promised Land. She had been very foolish in her thinking.

Mulvane watched the wagon rolling back toward the grove, and then he cut across the plain in the direction of Rawdon. This has not been a real test, he thought. The nesters in the grove had come a long way, and they had nothing to go back to. They were not going to give up so easily.

Back in town he unsaddled the claybank, had his late dinner, and then sat at one of the tables in the Alabama Bar for the remainder of the afternoon, playing solitaire.

The ranchers, he knew, were keeping a close eye on the grove, and they would keep him informed as to what was happening. They would know where to find him, too, and there was nothing for him to do now, but wait. It seemed like all his life he was waiting—maybe waiting for that bullet which would bring him down into the dust.

Chapter 4

L ate in the afternoon Sheriff Ed Bagley dropped in to see him—that same greasy smile on his face. As he pulled up a chair at Mulvane's table, he said:

"One o' them damned nesters came in to see me a few minutes ago. Claimed you figured on shootin' his mules. That right, Mulvane?"

Mulvane just looked at him and went on setting out the cards on the table.

"Asked him if he had any proof," Bagley chuckled, unabashed. "How many witnesses outside his own family, which don't count in court. Then I told him to get to hell out before I threw him out." He laughed, his chubby shoulders shaking, and then he added thoughtfully, "Nice lookin' little gal was with him, though, waitin' outside."

Mulvane looked up at him under the brim of his hat. "Stay away from her," he said softly.

Ed Bagley looked at him, a sly grin on his face. "That the way it is, Mulvane?" he chuckled. "Sure I'll stay away from her."

Mulvane paid no more attention to him, and after awhile Bagley walked over to the bar for

45

a beer, and then left. Mulvane pitied the nesters trying to secure justice through a man like that, but then they had no right to justice, nor anything else in this country.

Toward evening he went up to the hotel room, called for some hot water to shave, and then shaved carefully and put on a clean shirt. He went downstairs, then, to the dining room, and sat at one of the tables facing the lobby door. He wondered whether Hannah Carrington really would have supper with him.

He had been seated at the table for about five minutes when she swept into the room, and seeing him at the table, came immediately toward him. He got up, and she took the chair on the opposite side of the table.

"I haven't ordered," he said. "Wondered if you'd come."

"No reason why we can't have a meal together," she smiled.

"No reason," Mulvane agreed.

Then they ordered, and they sat at the table, looking across at each other.

Mulvane said quietly, "You wanted to see me about something, Miss Carrington?"

Hannah nodded, a faint smile on her face. "I thought you would guess it," she said. "There has been something on my mind, and I had a reason for wanting to see you tonight."

"You're worried about the nesters?" he asked.

"That's part of it," Hannah admitted. "I'm in the Association, and of course I want to see them kept out. I also voted to bring you in here to see that they were kept out, but there's something else."

Mulvane nodded. He'd had the feeling most of the afternoon that this was to be more than just a social engagement. He saw the worry in her eyes. "I'm listening," he said. He took a cigar from his vest pocket, and placed it on the table in front of him, intending to smoke it after the meal.

"It's about Ward Bryant," Hannah said slowly. "I'm kind of worried about him."

"Reckon he can take care of himself," Mulvane observed. "You figure on marrying him?"

Hannah Carrington frowned. "I don't know," she confessed. "We have never talked marriage, and he's only been back a short while."

"I'm listening," Mulvane said again.

Hannah took a deep breath. "It's odd," she said, "that I should talk to you about this, but you seem to be a man who is able to keep a confidence, especially if you are paid for the assignment."

Mulvane looked at her. "There's pay in this?" he asked.

"I'll tell you what it is, first," she told him. "Ward is a member of the Cattleman's Association, and he voted with the rest of us to bring you here to prevent the nesters from coming on to our ranges. He runs Rocking Chair, which next

47

to my own spread, is one of the biggest ranches in the county. He seems to be as anxious as anyone to rid this place of the nesters, but—" She hesitated, and Mulvane waited for her to go on.

"On two separate occasions," Hannah said slowly, "I know that he met with this Arno Quill, who is head of the emigrant group."

Mulvane stared. "Why would he meet with Quill?" he asked.

Hannah shook her head. "That's why I'm coming to you," she said. "I saw them the first time over at the old abandoned Whiting place at the north end of Ward's range. I came upon them by accident; I was not spying upon them. Ward had been talking with Quill, but when I came up Ward made no mention of his having seen Quill. He did not know that I had seen them together."

"There was a second time," Mulvane said.

"The second time," Hannah explained, "was in the hotel here. Quill, I believe has a room on the ground floor a few doors from mine. I came in to Rawdon unexpectedly last week, and when I went to my room I passed Mr. Quill's door, and I distinctly heard Ward's voice inside. I could not hear what they were speaking about, and I did not wish to listen, but they had been together."

"Ever see them together in public?" Mulvane asked.

Hannah shook her head. "That's the strange part about it," she said. "I've seen Ward pass

Quill on the street, and not even look at him, or notice him. As far as anyone could see they were total strangers."

Mulvane leaned back in the chair. "What is it you want me to do?" he asked.

"You're working for the Association," Hannah said. "You will be moving around this part of the country quite a bit. I want you to keep your ears and eyes open, and especially to watch Mr. Quill. Of course, I'll pay for this service."

Mulvane looked down at his hands and smiled. "I take money only for one job at a time," he stated.

Hannah looked at him curiously.

"Quill is working with the nesters," Mulvane went on, "and I would be keeping an eye on him, anyway." He paused, and then he said, "You, of course, have some idea as to what Bryant is up to. You've been thinking about this."

Hannah nodded. "I have a theory. It's not very sound, but it's the only thing I can go on. I can't think of Ward doing this, but there has to be a reason for his meeting with Quill."

"You figure he's selling out to the nesters," Mulvane murmured.

Hannah Carrington frowned. "What would you think?" she asked.

He shrugged. "It would be a good deal for the nesters," he said, "if they could get an open range like Rocking Chair. No one could drive

49

them out because they'd be on land which they owned. From there it would only be a matter of time before they began to spread out, and attract others to this country."

"I can't understand how Ward would want to do anything like that," Hannah murmured. "He's been away a number of years, and I know he's changed."

"I'll watch him," Mulvane promised.

"I hate to do this behind Ward's back," Hannah told him, "but don't see that I have any choice. Ward undoubtedly is planning something, and he's taken none of us into his confidence."

While they were eating a short while later, Hannah said, "I really would like to pay you for this, Mr. Mulvane."

Mulvane shook his head. "No pay," he said.

He sat there in the chair, vaguely conscious of the fact that he was disappointed. Hannah Carrington had wanted to see him because she had a proposition to make to him. He wondered how he could have been so foolish as to think that she wanted to meet him for social reasons.

It was good to know, though, that Ward Bryant was not in as solidly with Hannah as Mulvane had thought he was. Then he wondered why he permitted these things to bother him. It did not matter either way because in a short while he would be riding away from here, looking for another job to do, another problem to buck.

He sat at the table, wondering where it would eventually take him.

Hannah was saying to him, "Why do you hate the nesters so, Mr. Mulvane?"

"Had my troubles with them," Mulvane said flatly.

Then he told her briefly of his father and his brother. Hannah listened quietly until he'd finished, and then she said, "I can understand how you feel, Mr. Mulvane." She added thoughtfully, "I suppose you realize we can't keep them out forever. Some day all of this land will be fenced in, and the nesters will have the rest."

"I'll hit them," Mulvane said, "everywhere I find them, and as long as I can."

"What about the future?" Hannah asked him.

Mulvane shook his head. He had no answer to that question.

As the meal progressed he learned a little about her, also. She'd inherited Box C from her father who'd passed away a year and a half ago, and she'd been running the ranch on her own ever since. She'd been brought up on the ranch, and she knew cattle as well as any cattleman.

When they'd finished supper Mulvane smoked his cigar, and they talked for a while before Hannah went up to her room. Then Mulvane went out to the porch. Taking a seat at the far end in the shadows, he finished his cigar, and watched the street.

After awhile he got up and moved down the street, glancing into the various saloons until he located Arno Quill in the Great Western. Quill was at the bar talking with two other men when Mulvane came in. The short man looked at him coldly, the hatred in his small eyes.

Mulvane took no notice of him as he had his drink at the bar. He did find himself wondering, however, how a man like Ward Bryant could have gotten mixed up with a weasel like Arno Quill. Undoubtedly, the two of them had cooked up something where both would stand to make a sizeable profit, and Hannah Carrington's theory seemed as logical as any.

Mulvane had been at the bar less than five minutes when a small rat-faced little man came in through the doors, his eyes coming to stop on Mulvane standing at the bar.

The small man was probably a rider for one of the local outfits. He wore big Mexican spurs which jangled as he walked across the room, heading down toward the far end of the bar.

As he passed the spot where Mulvane was standing he slowed down, and he said softly, "John Harder wants to see you in the lodge hall now."

Then he walked on again, coming to a stop at the end of the bar. He had slanted, oriental eyes, dark in color, and his mouth was pulled down at the right side.

Mulvane watched him order a beer, and then he finished his own drink, paid for it, and left the Great Western, wondering what Harder had in mind.

The evening had turned slightly colder after the warmth of the day, and Mulvane had put on his leather jacket before stepping out into the night. He buttoned the jacket about his neck now as he headed up the street toward the Alabama Bar and the lodge hall above it.

He noticed as he left the Great Western that Quill was still there, chatting with his friends at the bar. The little man who'd brought the message had taken his beer and walked over to one of the tables to watch a card game.

Reaching the stairs, Mulvane went up, his boots making the wooden treads squeak as he walked. He wondered if Ward Bryant would be at this meeting, and then he remembered that Hannah had stated that Bryant had gone out to Rocking Chair that afternoon.

The door at the head of the stairs was closed when Mulvane reached the landing, but turning the knob he found it open. As he pushed in the door and stepped inside he stopped suddenly. The room was in complete darkness, unlike the other night when several of the overhead lamps had been lighted.

Mulvane stood framed in the doorway for a fraction of a second, and then he lunged to the left, dropping to the floor, his right hand slipping the Colt .44 from the holster.

Even as he fell, a gun roared in the room from a point not more than ten feet away. He saw the orange flame dart out at him wickedly, and he felt the tug of the lead as it grazed his leather jacket.

As his body hit the floor, he fired one shot at the flash of the gun, and he heard a man cry out softly. He knew that his bullet had gone home. Mulvane lay on the floor on his side, the gun still in his hand, listening carefully, holding his fire. By firing again now he would reveal his position on the floor.

As he lay there he could hear a man moving, his boots dragging. The man who'd tried to shoot him was breathing heavily and with difficulty. The bootsteps moved toward the far end of the darkened lodge hall away from him, and then he heard a heavy object fall to the floor, and he was positive the killer had dropped his gun.

He was sure now that he'd hit his man, and very hard. A man did not drop his gun in a gunfight unless he realized that the fight was over for him. Only one gun had opened up on him in the room, which meant that there had been only one killer waiting for him in this darkened room.

As the footsteps receded toward the other end of the long room, Mulvane got up slowly, the hammer of his gun pulled back. The man down at the other end of the room seemed to be stumbling now, lurching like a drunken man, his boots heavy on the wooden floor. Then, very suddenly Mulvane heard a loud crashing of glass, and he remembered that there had been two windows at the far end of the hall, and the killer had undoubtedly stumbled through one of them.

Moving down through the darkened room, Mulvane could see the dim shadow of the two windows, and the one on the left had been ripped out, sash and all. Looking out through the opening, he saw a man lying face downward on a low shed roof about three feet below the window ledge. It was dark back here at the rear of the street, but there was sufficient starlight for him to see the man quite clearly.

Holstering his gun, Mulvane picked out a few pieces of jagged glass, and then stepped through the opening to the roof below. The killer was sprawled, head and arms toward the rim of the roof and the back yard behind the lodge hall.

Bending down to roll the man over, he struck a match, holding it close to the man's face, and was surprised to learn that that snap shot fired at random in the darkness had gone all the way home. The man who'd waited for him in the lodge hall, a loaded gun in his hand, was dead.

He was a man of medium height with a blond mustache and a thin, straight mouth. Mulvane had looked into the faces of professional killers before, and he recognized the type. This man was a killer—cold, calculating, merciless, without nerves. Men who lived by the gun had the mark of it on their faces.

The bullet had gone through his chest, and a trickle of blood was now coming from his nose and mouth. He did not remember ever having seen this man in Rawdon, but that was not unusual. He knew very few people in this town. The killer could have been any one of a half hundred men he'd seen at the different bars along the street.

From the other end of the lodge hall he could hear a man calling, and he recognized Ed Bagley's voice. The shots had drawn men to the hall, and the sheriff of Rawdon was back at the doorway, hesitant about coming in. He was calling:

"Who in hell is that?"

Mulvane climbed back into the lodge hall, his eyes better accustomed to the darkness now. He located one of the hanging lamps, and striking a match he touched it to the wick, and then as the lamp took hold he shook the match out, tossed it away, and walked down toward the door.

Bagley came into the room, looking at him curiously, and he said:

"You fire that shot, Mulvane?"

Mulvane brushed by him, calling back over his shoulder, "Find a dead man out on that shed roof in the rear."

Then he went down the stairs hurriedly,

pushing his way through the crowd at the foot of the stairs, and he moved rapidly to the Great Western Saloon.

A little rat-faced man with big Mexican spurs, had sent him up those stairs to his death, and Mulvane had a bullet in his six-gun specially for the messenger.

When he pushed in through the bat-wing doors, however, he noticed that the messenger was gone. The saloon was nearly empty, too, most of the drinkers having gone out into the street when the guns went off.

Mulvane hooked a finger at the bartender who had served him, and when the man came up, he said quietly, "Thin-faced man in a brown vest, black hat, was drinking at this end of the bar. You see him?"

The bartender wiped the bar with his rag. "Saw him leave a little while after you did, mister," he said.

"You know him?" Mulvane asked.

The bartender shook his head. "New one to me," he stated.

Mulvane was convinced that the man was speaking the truth. He went out again into the street, and he stood out in front of the Great Western watching the men coming back from the lodge hall. He waited until Bagley came down the stairs, pompous as usual, as if he'd gunned a man, himself.

As Bagley came up the street, Mulvane could hear him dispatching a man for the coroner, and then as Bagley reached the Great Western Mulvane said to him, "Who was he?"

Bagley pulled up, pushing his hat back on his head. "Feller on the roof?" he asked.

"You know damned well," Mulvane snapped. "Who was he?"

"Don't know him," Bagley said. "Must be some drifter ridin' through this way."

Mulvane laughed tonelessly. "A drifter sent a man with a message to meet me up at the lodge hall, and then waited for me with a gun. What the hell kind of drifter is that?"

Bagley shrugged. "He throw the first shot, Mulvane?"

"You know it," Mulvane scowled.

Bagley frowned. "Reckon I don't know why," he stated blandly. "That one's a new one to me."

Mulvane couldn't tell whether the sheriff was lying or not. He had his own theory about the attempted killing. Once before nesters had banded together and brought in a hired killer to take care of him, and possibly the group in the grove had done the same thing. It was only a theory, however, and he found it difficult to accept the fact that the farmers in the grove had gone this far.

That left one other theory. The dead man on the

shed roof would never talk again, and could never explain who had sent him, but he had been sent because Mulvane was interfering with someone's plans, and if Hannah Carrington were right, Ward Bryant had a plan.

Chapter 5

In the morning Mulvane came down as usual for his breakfast. Stepping into the dining room, he took his seat at the other end of the room. He did not look up when the girl came over to wait on him, and he said, "Ham and eggs. Coffee with them."

The girl said, laughingly, "Don't you know me, Mr. Mulvane?"

He looked up quickly into the twinkling brown eyes of Ruby Watkins. She was wearing a new dress, and an apron over the dress, and her hair was done up prettily in a bunch at the back.

Mulvane stared at her for a moment, and then he said, "What are you doing here, Ruby?"

"I work here," Ruby smiled. "Got the job yesterday afternoon, and I started this morning."

"What about your uncle?" Mulvane asked, mystified.

"I've left them," Ruby said casually. "Uncle Joab cursed me yesterday because I couldn't help him get his land. We've had trouble before, and now I've had enough of him."

Mulvane frowned. "You'll be living at the hotel, then?" he asked.

Ruby nodded. "I guess, if you want," she said with that child-like innocence, "we can be seeing each other a little more."

Mulvane saw Hannah Carrington coming into the dining room, and when she saw him with Ruby, she walked on to another table, nodding her good morning to him. He wondered if she would have sat down at his table if Ruby had not been there, and he was a little annoyed with the nester girl because of this.

"You figure on staying in this town now?" Mulvane asked Ruby.

"I have a job here," Ruby told him. "I'm making some money, and I have a place to live. Mr. Wolsey, who owns the hotel, seems like a nice man, and he's had a hard time keeping girls." She laughed, and she added, "This is better than living in a wagon or a sod shanty."

Mulvane nodded, "You could be better off here," he agreed.

Ruby said before she left to get his order, "I hear there's a dance on Friday night in town. Would you be going, Mr. Mulvane?"

Mulvane looked at her. "Didn't come here to dance," he said.

Ruby looked disappointed. "If you go," she said, "you might see me there, anyway."

Mulvane didn't answer, as he watched her walking away, head erect, completely composed, her dress swishing around her. He noticed that she still wore the same old shoes.

He sat at his table, and Hannah Carrington sat at a table about fifteen feet away. It seemed very foolish of them to sit this way after having dined together the night before, and he having made a promise to her that he would try to help her in her difficulties with Ward Bryant.

On an impulse, Mulvane got up and walked over to her table, pulling out a chair. He sat down across from her, and he said, "You heard about last night?"

"I heard someone tried to kill you," Hannah stated. "Did you know the man?"

"Somebody put a killer on my tail," he growled, "and this town damn near saw the last of me last night."

Hannah looked at him across the table. "You have any enemies in this town?"

Mulvane laughed mirthlessly. "Nineteen nester wagons in the grove, alone," he said, "and every one of them would breathe easier if I were dead, and then there's Quill. He owes me one, too."

Hannah was watching him carefully, her blue eyes fixed on his. "And who else?" she asked.

Mulvane shrugged. "Who knows?" he smiled grimly. "Anybody who stands to profit by these nesters moving out on to the cattle ranges."

"Ward Bryant," Hannah said without any emotion. "If he's in with the nesters he would be anxious to have you out of the way."

Mulvane put both hands down flat on the table. "It's an idea," he agreed, and he wondered why she'd brought it up. He said, "You mind if I have my breakfast with you. Wanted to hear what you thought about this affair last night."

Hannah nodded. "What were you doing in the lodge hall last night?" she asked.

Mulvane told her about the message he'd received, and how he'd walked into the darkened lodge hall.

"No one seems to know either the man who brought the message, or the man I shot," he said. "They both could have been brought here for this particular job."

Hannah frowned. She watched Ruby Watkins coming up with the coffee Mulvane had ordered. As Ruby set it down on the table in front of him, the nester girl said, "What will you have, ma'am?"

Hannah gave her order, and when Ruby had gone away, the ranch woman said, "I notice your little lady friend from the grove is now in town."

Mulvane felt the color come to his face. "I didn't bring her here," he snapped.

"She's a very pretty girl," Hannah observed, "and she likes you."

"Should I be pleased?" Mulvane asked.

Hannah smiled at him across the table. "Most men would be pleased if a pretty girl were infatuated with them," she said.

"She'll find plenty of men friends in this town," he observed.

Arno Quill was coming into the room now for his breakfast, and he gave Mulvane a cold stare as he passed by on the other side.

Hannah said, "He could have sent those killers after you, Mr. Mulvane."

Mulvane nodded. Quill hated him enough to do it, but he didn't think Quill had the nerve to actually arrange for a man's murder.

Having his breakfast with Hannah Carrington, Mulvane knew what he would do that morning. He owed Ward Bryant a visit.

He said to Hannah, "Heading out to the ranch this morning?"

Hannah nodded. "Thought I'd ride back," she said. "What about you?"

"Might visit some of the ranchers," he told her. "Reckon there'll be somebody watching that grove all the time."

Hannah nodded. "John Harder made arrangements for that," she told him.

When they'd finished eating, she went back to her room, and Mulvane stepped around to the stable to saddle the claybank. Five minutes later he was riding out of Rawdon, heading west.

He wondered what he would do if he were to find the little rat-faced man out at Rocking Chair. If Bryant had been behind this bushwhack scheme then the man who had brought the message in the Great Western could still be in the vicinity, hiding out at Rocking Chair.

Mulvane moved along without any particular haste, passing John Harder's Circle H spread, and the ranch of another member of the Association, before reaching Rocking Chair.

Coming up on the Rocking Chair spread, he had to pass a sprawling meadow, a long bunkhouse, capable of holding fifteen or twenty riders, a number of corrals, and then the ranchhouse beyond, a log affair with a verandah running the entire width of the house, and most of it partly concealed by tall cottonwoods.

Several men lounged near the front of the bunkhouse door, smoking, and they turned to watch as he rounded one of the corrals. Mulvane recognized Jud Faraday, the Rocking Chair ramrod. Faraday was leaning against the wall of the bunkhouse, and he tossed the cigarette away when Mulvane came up, nodding and smiling at Mulvane. It was a hard, tough smile, though, with no friendliness in it.

"Bryant around?" Mulvane asked.

"Off up at the north range," Faraday told him.

Mulvane looked at the two men with Faraday, and then at the bunkhouse door. There was that challenging smile on Faraday's face, and cold humor deep down in his yellowish eyes.

"Looking for somebody, Mulvane?" Faraday grinned.

"I could be," Mulvane told him.

"Hear somebody had you set up in the lodge hall last night," Faraday went on. "Reckon this town's tougher than you figured, mister."

"When they fire at a man in the darkness," Mulvane said, "they're not tough; they're dirty."

Faraday shrugged. "Reckon you got your man," he observed, "and he didn't get you."

Mulvane looked at him. "One of them got away," he stated. "That's the one I'm after."

Faraday lifted his eyebrows. "Here?" he asked.

"Anywhere," Mulvane told him. "Anywhere I can find him. You vouch for all the riders you have at Rocking Chair?"

Faraday hooked his hands in his gunbelt, and stood in front of the claybank, rocking back and forth. "Riders come an' go," he said. "Some we got for a week, an' they're gone. Others been around here, I guess, for years."

"Anybody in that bunkhouse?" Mulvane asked.

Faraday said over his shoulder, "Go see, Marty."

One of the men with him turned to step into the bunkhouse, and Mulvane said, "Hold it up, Marty."

The Rocking Chair rider paused, looking first at Mulvane, then at Jud Faraday. Mulvane was dismounting now, and he said to Faraday, "Reckon I'll have a look, myself."

As he started to move around the Rocking Chair

ramrod, Faraday shifted over in front of him. The tough little ranch foreman was still smiling, but his eyes were narrowed.

"I run this outfit for Ward Bryant," he said. "I give the orders around here, Mulvane."

"You might give one too many," Mulvane told him. "You tell your boy to stay away from that bunkhouse. Some dog threw lead at me last night in the dark, and I aim to find his friend."

Faraday shook his head slowly, and Mulvane could not tell whether he was shielding someone, or just being plain stubborn about his position at Rocking Chair.

Mulvane said, "I'm going in there, Faraday. Move away."

"Like hell," Faraday grinned.

Mulvane knew, then, that he had no choice. Both men seemed to realize at the same time that it was useless to waste words. As Mulvane tried to go around him, Faraday lunged forward, swinging with his right fist. He was a tremendously powerful little man who could have given Mulvane a rough time of it, but Mulvane stepped away from the blow, sliding his gun from the holster at the same time, and slashing the barrel down across the front of Faraday's skull. The Rocking Chair ramrod collapsed on the ground and lay without moving.

Mulvane walked around him, and the Rocking Chair rider who had been in the doorway, moved to one side to let him pass. He kicked in the door, the gun still in his hand, and looked inside.

The long room was empty, but there was another door at the far end which could have permitted his man to escape—if he'd been in the bunkhouse, and listening to the talk outside.

Walking through the bunkhouse to the other end, Mulvane opened the door and looked out. The rear of the bunkhouse faced toward the main ranchhouse another fifteen or twenty yards away.

Going back to the front of the bunkhouse he stepped outside, finding Jud Faraday climbing unsteadily to his feet, and then he saw Ward Bryant swinging toward him from the direction of one of the stables. Mulvane didn't know whether Bryant had just ridden in, or Faraday had been lying about Bryant's being away.

"What the hell goes on here?" Bryant snapped.

Faraday was still too dazed to talk. Mulvane said, "Figured I'd have a look in that bunkhouse. Your man figured I wouldn't."

"What's your business in my bunkhouse?" Bryant grated.

Mulvane looked at him. "Some dog tried to kill me last night. Figured I'd have a look around here, and everywhere else."

"You won't find anything here," Bryant told him grimly. "Now get the hell out."

Mulvane smiled. "Ready to go," he said.

He rode off, then, leaving Ward Bryant glaring

after him. A single thought was running through his mind all the while—if there had been a man hiding in the bunkhouse he could have left by that rear door, and stepped into the main ranch-house without being seen.

He could be hiding out there now, but Mulvane realized that if he insisted upon making a search of the house, Bryant would definitely draw a gun on him. He wasn't sure of Ward Bryant yet, and gun play would not solve anything.

He rode on making a circuit of some of the ranches, and on the way back to Rawdon he stopped at the Harder ranchhouse, finding John Harder out. He moved on down to town, coming back the middle of the afternoon, and he turned the claybank into the stable behind the hotel.

He said to the hostler back there, "Miss Carrington leave for her ranch?"

"Left," the man told him, "an hour or so ago."

Leaving the stable, Mulvane want back to the street. Sheriff Ed Bagley was sitting on the porch as Mulvane went up the hotel steps. Bagley hopped out of his chair, seeing Mulvane, and came toward him, motioning for Mulvane to pull up.

The lawman of Rawdon had a cigar in his mouth, and he threw away the stub as he came forward. Mulvane waited for him impatiently near the doorway.

"More trouble down in that damned grove,"

69

Bagley said. "Hear them nesters are bringin' in a U.S. marshal. That's the talk Arno Quill is makin' around this town now. Tell me he's on the way to Rawdon now."

Mulvane looked down at his dusty boots. Bagley was trying to appear concerned over the matter, but Mulvane was quite sure he saw a triumphant gleam in the fat man's amber eyes.

"How you figure on handling this?" Bagley asked.

"You're the law in this town," Mulvane told him.

Bagley did grin now. "I was the law," he chuckled, "reckon I'd have to run you out, Mulvane, an' let them damned nesters take over the range. Reckon that's right, ain't it?"

"You're a poor excuse for the law." Mulvane told him, "You're not even a man, Bagley."

Even this did not seem to ruffle the fat man. He tugged at his black mustache with one of his flabby hands, and he said, "Save the tough talk for the nesters and the marshal, Mulvane. What I want to know is what you figure on doin' about it."

"Wait until he gets here," Mulvane said.

He went on into the lobby of the hotel. He wasn't sure, himself, what he was going to do about the U.S. marshal coming into the territory. It would be difficult fighting the law of the land, but even this was not a new twist in the game which he was playing against the nesters. Once before a group of nesters had banded together to bring in a U.S. marshal, but Mulvane had no difficulty with the man because the wealthy ranchers had bought him out even before he'd arrived on the scene.

He wondered, though, how this man would be handled, and he realized now that they were beginning to crowd him in Rawdon. Ward Bryant, he thought, wanted him dead; the nesters in the grove wanted him out of the way, too, and now they were using the United States Government to do it. Sooner or later, one or the other would have to catch up with him.

Chapter 6

Mulvane had more trouble in store for him that afternoon, though, and from an unexpected source. Joab Watkin's, Ruby's uncle, rode up to the hotel late afternoon as Mulvane was reading the newspaper on the porch. The nester was alone, and obviously quite mad about something.

Seeing Mulvane on the porch he pulled up and pointed a bony finger at him. He said, his voice quivering with emotion, "Comin' in here to take my girl back to the grove, mister. You're the one got her to come here in the first place."

Mulvane slid his boots from the porch railing to the floor. He said flatly, "I had nothing to do with it, but I'm damned glad she came. She's better off living by herself than in a wagon with you."

"Then why don't you marry her?" Watkins almost shouted, his thin face working.

Mulvane got up from the chair, and Joab Watkins, who had come up on the porch and was walking toward the door, backed away quickly.

"You ain't workin' me over, mister," he said, and he hurried into the hotel lobby.

Mulvane followed him, frowning, not sure just what the nester could do. If Ruby Watkins were not of age he could possibly force her to go back with him until she was.

Entering the lobby, Mulvane found that Joab Watkins had gone on back into the kitchen. He could hear loud voices back there, and then Ruby came running through the dining room. When she saw Mulvane in the doorway of the lobby she headed toward him, her face white.

"I'm not going back," she sobbed. "I'm not going back with him. Please don't let him take me."

Joab and the harassed hotel owner—a little man with a bald head by the name of Wolsey—came out of the kitchen. Joab was saying triumphantly, "She has to go back. She's not of age. Feller down at the grove told me that."

Ruby stood beside Mulvane. He could see her shoulders trembling.

"How old are you?" he asked her.

"Eighteen," she said. "I'm not going back, Mr. Mulvane."

"Has to be twenty-one out this way to be on her own," Watkins was grinning. "Now you come along with me, girl."

Mr. Wolsey was saying, "She's a good girl. She does her work well. She can stay here and work as long as she wants to for my part. Maybe we'd better get Sheriff Bagley over here."

"Not him!" Joab Watkins whooped. "I've had enough o' that one, too."

"Reckon you'd better clear out," Mulvane said. "This girl doesn't want to live with you, and there's no way you can force her in this town."

"Circuit judge comes here in the fall," Mr. Wolsey said. "If you have any complaints you can make them then, Mr. Watkins."

"I want to stay," Ruby said again.

Joab Watkins snarled at Mulvane, "It's all your fault, mister. You talked her into this."

"Get out," Mulvane snapped.

Joab left, knowing that he could do nothing more now, and when he'd gone Ruby said to Mulvane, "I'm obliged to you, Mr. Mulvane."

"Just do your work," he told her. "You'll be all right here."

He went out to the porch again, and he sat down, disgruntled with the whole mess. It seemed as if he were constantly getting mixed up with the nester girl, and always against his will. He wondered if it would be wise for him to give her some of the five hundred dollars he'd received from the ranchmen, and put her on a train back to Indiana, but then he realized that she probably had no one there who wanted her.

He sat there on the porch the remainder of the afternoon, watching the darkness come on. It was in the night that they waited for him in the back alleys, behind darkened windows, and in doorways.

He could recall at least half a dozen separate times when he'd been shot at from ambush. Twice he'd been wounded slightly, and now another man was loose in this town, or somewhere close by, a man who had been paid to kill him, whose partner had been shot down the previous night up at the lodge hall.

Mulvane got up from the chair, stretched, and then took a turn up the street, walking to the last house, and then turning around and starting back again. He saw people watching him as he walked. They all knew him now, and feared him. He was not their kind, and they knew it, but there was nothing they could do with him.

He was in one sense neither a blessing nor a curse to this town which watched tacitly this battle between the nesters and the ranch men. They probably preferred the ranchers who spent more money, and whose riders came into this town for the same purpose.

The evening came on swiftly, and Mulvane stepped into the hotel for his evening meal. Ruby Watkins waited on him again, very pleased to be able to do so.

She chattered continuously as he ordered his meal, and she reminded him of a small bird chirping away merrily without a care in the world. He had never met a girl like this before.

She was penniless, and was having trouble with her relations; she had no friends in this town, yet she seemed to be completely unafraid.

Again, he found himself comparing her with Hannah Carrington. Hannah was invariably cool, poised, with a ready, calculating mind. She spoke unhurriedly, and always when she spoke he got the impression that she was not completely unburdening herself to him as Ruby Watkins was now.

"I'm going to save my money," Ruby was saying. "I need some new clothes, and I need shoes, and I want to fix up my room at the back of the hotel. It's not very big, but it's very comfortable, and I like it. It's all my own."

Then she went off on a new topic, and Mulvane listened to her, amazed at the way her mind jumped around from one subject to another.

"You won't go to the dance with me Friday?" she asked.

"Plenty of young men you can get in this town," Mulvane told her.

"I'd rather go with you," she said. "You're the only friend I have in Rawdon, Mr. Mulvane." She paused, and she laughed, then she went on, "I know that you don't like the nesters, but I'm not a nester any more."

Mulvane smiled at her. "This dance is for Friday, which is three days away," he said. "I could be dead in three days."

Ruby shook her head in exasperation. "Why don't you leave this business?" she asked him. "You don't have to do it. Why don't you get married, and if you don't like to farm, you could raise stock."

Mulvane chuckled. "Who would I marry?" he asked.

"You could marry me," she said. "I would marry you tonight, Mr. Mulvane."

"You're crazy," Mulvane told her. "Now get me my supper."

She was smiling at him as she went back to the kitchen.

After eating, he went up to his room, checked his gun carefully, and came down a little while later. As he went past the dining room Ruby Watkins stepped to the doorway and said to him, "Please be careful tonight."

Mulvane thought about that as he went out into the night. Careful men died quickly. The men who did not give a damn lived forever it seemed. He'd always been the other kind, and nothing had ever happened to him. Were he to start worrying about his life now, he knew he wouldn't last very long. He had the edge on other men because he didn't care, and he was loose where they were tight and worried.

Passing some of the saloons he noted that the usual number of nesters had come up from the grove, and there were some riders in from the ranches. Out in front of the Great Western Saloon he saw Ward Bryant's big bay horse, and Faraday's dapple gray was there, also, standing three-legged at the tie rack, the Rocking Chair brand on the hip.

Looking in over the doors, he saw Bryant and Faraday at the bar, and farther down along the same bar he spotted Arno Quill. This, he decided, was the place where he would spend his evening. This was the nerve center of Rawdon tonight, and instinctively Mulvane headed for it.

As he pushed in through the doors he saw Ward Bryant turn to look at him, and then Faraday turned, also, and Mulvane could see the anger start up in the short man's yellow eyes.

Faraday had his senses now, and he was thinking of that gun-whipping he'd taken from Mulvane out at the ranch. Mulvane was sure that tonight the squat man would try to even the score. He wondered if Bryant had deliberately brought in the fiery-tempered Faraday just for this purpose.

Mulvane had a word to say to Bryant, and he headed straight for the bar, pulling up next to the Rocking Chair owner. He stood there, his head turned slightly toward Bryant, and he said, "Hear the nesters are bringing in a United States marshal."

"What about it?" Bryant snapped.

Mulvane smiled at him coolly. "I don't fight the

United States Government," he said. "What does the Cattleman's Association aim to do?"

"Damned if I know," Bryant growled.

Mulvane touched the shirt pocket in which he still carried the check he'd received from the Association. He said easily, "Some of your money's in this pocket, Bryant. That mean anything to you?"

"You came here to do a job," Bryant said grimly. "Go ahead and do it."

"I don't buck the government," Mulvane repeated. "You boys handle the government and I'll take care of the nesters."

"Tell it to Harder," Ward Bryant said casually.

"You don't care?" Mulvane asked him.

"I don't give a damn," Bryant snapped. "Now let me finish my drink."

Mulvane shrugged and pulled away from him. He'd sounded his man out, and he'd learned what he had to know. Bryant wasn't too anxious to see the nesters driven away.

Jud Faraday said slowly as Mulvane moved past him, "There ain't a man in this part of the country, Mulvane, can gun-whip me, and get away with it."

"I got away with it," Mulvane told him, smiling.

"Next time you use that gun," Faraday said softly, "use it the right way."

"I know how to do that, too," Mulvane nodded.

79

"Ask that dog who tried to get me up in the lodge hall last night."

He walked on, then, knowing that Faraday was watching him, and he sat down at one of the card games where he could keep an eye on the door and on Faraday at the same time.

He played several hands with the men at the table, all of whom were a little uneasy in his presence.

As he sat at the table he saw Sheriff Bagley come in, smiling, affable as usual—the complete politician—his black mustache waxed and looking almost artificial. Bagley had a word or two with Bryant at the bar, had a look over at Mulvane at the card table, and then left a little while later, apparently to make his rounds of the town.

Mulvane watched Jud Faraday drinking steadily at the bar, building up his hate, and he wondered how long it would be before the Rocking Chair ramrod figured he was fired up enough to make his play. There was still a question in Mulvane's mind as to how far Faraday would go tonight, with guns or with fists, but one way or the other he was positive Faraday would have it out.

Mulvane watched men coming in and going out of the Great Western as the news spread through the town that Jud Faraday was on the prod for the Cattleman's Association's hired gun.

Within thirty minutes after Mulvane had

entered the saloon it was filled to capacity. He was confident that the other saloons in town were comparatively empty. Excitement had drawn this crowd into the Great Western the way a piece of raw meat draws flies.

From the card table Mulvane watched Faraday, recognizing him as a man who could take plenty of strong liquor, and yet the drink would have little effect upon him, physically. With a dozen or more shots under his belt, Faraday would be as tough as a man perfectly sober, and a lot more dangerous.

It was about ten-thirty when the Rocking Chair ramrod decided it was time. Somewhere deep back in the inner recesses of the squat man's mind, a bell rang, indicating that the time had arrived for him to avenge that gun-whipping.

Watching him from under the brim of his hat, Mulvane played his cards, keeping his face expressionless. When he saw Faraday leave the bar and head in his direction he did not even bother to look up. He noticed, though, that it had become very quiet in the Great Western, and one of the men at his table suddenly got up and walked away without saying a word.

The Rocking Chair ramrod stopped a few feet from where Mulvane sat, and he said slowly, "On your feet, Mulvane."

Mulvane put his cards down on the table and looked up. He could see Ward Bryant at the bar watching them, a cold grin on Bryant's face. Evidently, Bryant had seen Faraday in action before, probably with his fists, and he was looking forward to this encounter.

The other two men at the table with Mulvane threw in their cards, then moved toward the far wall of the room.

Mulvane said easily, "What do you want, Faraday?"

"You know damn well what I want," Faraday rasped. "On your feet, mister."

"You could have had it before," Mulvane smiled. "You have to stoke up on liquor, Faraday?"

"On your feet," Faraday snapped again.

Mulvane got up, pushing the chair back behind him.

The bartender was saying worriedly from the other side of the bar, "Why not take it outside, gentlemen? No call to wreck my place."

"Go to hell," Faraday said over his shoulder. "You made enough money on me, George." Then he said to Mulvane, "Take off your gunbelt, mister." He unbuckled his and draped it on the bar. "We'll see how tough you are without it."

Mulvane shrugged and unbuckled the belt, placing it on the card table. Faraday didn't want it with guns, so this was the way it had to be. There were other ways of fighting a man like Faraday aside from using the fists.

82

Ward Bryant said from the bar, "Jump him, Jud."

Faraday went into action coming in low and fast, diving for Mulvane's waist, and seeking to throw him to the floor.

Anticipating that the short man would try to close with him immediately, Mulvane was ready. As he stood waiting for Faraday to make his move he had one hand resting on the back of the chair upon which he'd been sitting, and snatching up the chair now he whirled it over his head and crashed it down hard across the top of Faraday's head and shoulders.

The chair disintegrated, and Faraday stumbled forward, still on his feet, but very dazed. As he lurched in, Mulvane brought his right knee up hard into Faraday's nose, smashing the bone, and drawing a short scream of pain from the Rocking Chair ramrod. Blood poured from both nostrils as Faraday's head was jerked upward.

Mulvane leaped in at him, slashing savagely with both fists to the face, driving his man back toward the bar. He had his man going now, and he would not let up until Faraday was through.

The short man, dazed and hurt badly with the broken nose, strove to fight back, but the fury of Mulvane's attack was too much for him. Mulvane moved him along the bar, pounding with his fists. Blood now came from Faraday's mouth, and from cuts around the eyes.

Ward Bryant had stepped aside to watch them, and he was touching a match to a cigar as Mulvane hammered away at the foreman. There was no expression on Bryant's face, neither disappointment, nor hatred. He was watching one of his men being beaten unmercifully, and it meant nothing to him. Mulvane saw on his face the same cool confidence he'd displayed from the first moment Mulvane had laid his eyes upon him.

Faraday fell to the floor once, but managed to climb up to the bar stupidly, gripping the foot rail, and then the edge of the bar with his hand. His eyes were beginning to glaze, and his face was a bloody mask. He looked for Mulvane, trying to make his eyes focus, but was unable to do so.

He was staggering, leaning on the bar, and then he turned his back full on Mulvane, and looked for him in the opposite direction.

"All right," he was mumbling. "All right."

He was in no condition to continue a fight, and Mulvane turned away from him, walking back to the table to buckle on his gun. As he passed Bryant who was watching him, he said, "Next time you do the jumping, mister."

"I might," Bryant grinned, "but not that way."

"Anyway you want it," Mulvane told him.

Bryant was still smiling as he turned and signalled for one of his riders to come up and give the dazed Jud Faraday a hand. The Rocking Chair man took Faraday by the arm, leading him out of the saloon, and Mulvane presumed, up toward the doctor's office to have the nose mended.

Bryant left a moment later as Mulvane stepped up to the bar for a drink, which he felt he needed badly after the fight. His hands were raw and bleeding from the contact with Faraday's hard face.

After downing his drink Mulvane went out into the street, remembering that there was still a possibility that the little rat-faced killer with the big Mexican spurs was still in town, waiting for him in some dark corner.

Walking back to the hotel, Mulvane gave all the alleys a wide berth, and as he moved past the darkened entrances of several stores he kept his hand on his gun. He had no trouble, however, and he entered the hotel.

The clerk had evidently stepped away from his desk for the moment, and Mulvane saw no one in the lobby as he started up the stairs. Then he heard Ruby Watkins calling after him softly, "Mr. Mulvane—Mr. Mulvane."

When he stopped she came up, looking at him closely. "You all right?" she asked. "I heard a man say that there was going to be a fight in the Great Western, and that you would be in it."

When she saw Mulvane's battered hands, she

let out a small cry of sympathy, and grasping one of the hands she looked at it closely.

"It's all right," he growled.

"They should be washed and bandaged," Ruby said quickly. "Please let me do it, Mr. Mulvane. There's warm water back in the kitchen, and I think I can find some bandaging."

"Just a few scratches," Mulvane tried to tell her.

"You need warm water and bandaging," Ruby insisted. "Please, Mr. Mulvane."

She held him by the arm, and he reluctantly let her lead him across the lobby, through the dining room, and into the big, empty hotel kitchen.

She had him sit down at a table as she scurried about getting a basin and pouring warm water into it. Then she disappeared, coming back in a few moments with some cloth for bandaging.

"Does it hurt?" she asked anxiously, as Mulvane put his hands gingerly into the basin.

Thinking about Jud Faraday's battered face and broken nose, Mulvane almost had to smile. He sat in the chair and Ruby washed the blood from his hands with a damp cloth. After awhile she dried his hands, and put bandages around the knuckles—bandages which Mulvane knew he would take off in the morning because they would surely interfere with his handling of a gun.

She took her time about the bandaging, seeming

to enjoy it, looking up at him occasionally as she worked, and she said, "Who were you fighting, Mr. Mulvane?"

"Ramrod from Rocking Chair," he told her, "a real tough one."

"Why must you always be fighting people?" Ruby asked slowly.

Thinking back, Mulvane said, "They started fighting me, and it just never ended." He did want to know, though, why he was fighting ranchmen in this particular case.

When Ruby had finished with his hands she patted them gently, and said, "If you'll just sit here, I'll pour you a cup of hot coffee. There's plenty on the stove."

"Reckon I can stand that," Mulvane nodded.

His hands did feel good, and he felt grateful to the nester girl who was so much interested in him. He watched her pour two cups of coffee from the pot on the stove, and then she came down and sat at the table with him.

As he sipped the coffee he said, "Don't worry about that uncle of yours. He can't do anything until a judge gets here in the fall, and by that time the nesters will be gone, and he'll be gone with them."

"I'll never go back with him," Ruby stated flatly.

"You'd be a fool to," Mulvane agreed.

Ruby said after awhile, "What are you going

to do after you drive my uncle and his people away?"

Mulvane shrugged. "I'm paid for this job," he said. "When this is over, I'll look for another one. Always been plenty to do."

They sat at the table, sipping coffee. Now, looking across at Ruby Watkins, Mulvane saw the warmth and the glow in her brown eyes. He said, "I'm obliged to you for fixing up my hands."

"I was glad to do it," Ruby told him. "This is the first time I've ever done anything for you."

Mulvane smiled. He could hear a clock ticking in the hotel kitchen, and he could hear water boiling gently on the stove. The coffee was very good, and he had a second cup, Ruby urging it upon him.

After she had poured him the second cup, she put the pot back on the stove, and she was walking around the table to her chair, when Mulvane put his hands out and took her arm. Then he stood up, drawing her close, and he kissed her.

She was at first surprised, almost startled by his action, not expecting it, but she responded immediately, and he could feel her hands tight on his arms.

When he finally released her, she stepped back, smiling at him, and she said softly, "I should think it was time, Mr. Mulvane."

Mulvane scowled and sat down.

"I'm glad you did it," Ruby told him. "If you were to marry me I wouldn't have any trouble with my uncle or anyone else."

"That the only reason you want to marry me?" Mulvane smiled.

"I'd want to marry you," she laughed, "even if I didn't have an uncle."

Mulvane looked at the cup on the table. He wasn't quite sure, himself, why he'd kissed the nester girl. It had been an impulse as she'd passed by. She had been kind, and she was highly attractive, and she was young, and they were alone.

"You'd be a fool," Mulvane told her, "tying yourself on to a man like me."

"I like you," Ruby smiled at him, "and that's enough for me. It wouldn't matter where we lived, or how we lived, as long as we lived together."

Mulvane stood up. "You'd better get these ideas out of your head. You're only a child."

"I'm glad you kissed me," Ruby said softly, "very glad, Mr. Mulvane."

Then she left him, going to her room off the kitchen. Mulvane went out into the dining room, and then to the lobby. Entering the lobby, he saw the clerk standing at the foot of the stairs, staring up.

Mulvane said to him, "Trouble?"

The clerk spun around, his watery eyes wide.

He gulped and pointed, and before he could say anything a gun roared, the sound filling the upper floor of the hotel.

Approaching the stairs, gun in hand now, Mulvane waited. The shot had come from the direction of his room, but it had not been aimed at him because his room was around a bend from the landing.

On the bottom step Mulvane waited. He could hear a man stumbling along the corridor, approaching the landing, and he said over his shoulder, "Who went up there?"

Before the clerk could reply, he had his answer. Jud Faraday came into sight, his battered nose bandaged with adhesive tape, his face horribly swollen and cut from the fight in the Great Western.

Faraday had a gun in his hand, but he was not going to use it. The gun drooped as the Rocking Chair ramrod reached the landing, and then it dropped to the floor. A moment later Faraday pitched forward down the stairs, his body striking each step with a sickening thud as he rolled and slid down to where Mulvane was standing.

Mulvane moved back to let him fall, and as Faraday's body rolled over so that he was lying on his back, Mulvane could see the flow of blood spreading out around what must have been a bullet hole in his stomach.

Leaping over the body, Mulvane went up the steps two at a time, the gun in his hand, knowing now what had happened. Faraday had come looking for him in the hotel room, with a gun this time, and he'd walked into a trap which had been set for Mulvane.

The killer had been concealed in Mulvane's room with a gun lined on the door, and as Faraday broke in, the ramrod had been shot down coldly without a word of warning.

Racing down the corridor to his open doorway, Mulvane hesitated before leaping through, and then he heard the shade flapping at the open window which he remembered distinctly he'd left closed when he'd gone out earlier this evening. Once again his man had fled.

Moving across the darkened room he came to the rear window and looked down, seeing nothing. The killer had thrown that single shot at Jud Faraday, and then had leaped through the window to the ground, a drop of a dozen or so feet. It was too late to search for the man, and Mulvane still didn't know who to look for. Possibly, Ward Bryant, or someone else had sent another killer after him.

Going back downstairs he found the frightened hotel clerk still standing near the body of Jud Faraday, and then he saw Ruby Watkins running into the lobby, her face white. When she saw him the relief came into her eyes.

Mulvane holstered his gun, and was bending down to have a look at Faraday when Sheriff Bagley came through the door. The sheriff moved over to the body and looked down, and then he said, "Reckon he should have been satisfied with that beating, Mulvane."

Mulvane just looked at the man, contempt in his eyes. Then the hotel clerk said hurriedly, "Mr. Mulvane didn't shoot him, Sheriff. He was down here when Faraday got it upstairs."

Ed Bagley stared at Mulvane curiously. "Who shot him?" he demanded.

"Ask him," Mulvane snapped, and he walked into the dining room, pushing Ruby Watkins ahead of him.

"They tried to shoot you," Ruby said slowly.

"And they missed again," Mulvane told her.

Chapter 7

Early the next morning Mulvane saw Hannah Carrington riding into town in her buckboard. He was having his hair cut in the barber shop across the way from the hotel when he saw the buckboard turning into the alley behind the hotel.

A few minutes later Hannah entered the hotel, and he wondered if she were looking for him. He leaned back in the barber chair watching the street as the barber cut his hair. When he came out of the barber shop he stopped in at the dry goods store to buy a clean shirt, and then he returned to the hotel finding Hannah sitting in the lobby and waiting impatiently. He wondered if she expected him to be at her beck and call all the time because she'd asked him to keep an eye on Ward Bryant.

Hannah was wearing a tanned leather jacket, and she was hatless, her brown hair done up in a ribbon. When Mulvane came over to sit down beside her, she said, "Hear you had a little trouble last night."

"Plenty," Mulvane told her. He didn't tell her what had happened because he realized that the story had undoubtedly reached Hannah

Carrington's ears not many hours after it had happened. "What brings you to town?" he asked.

"I understand there's a United States marshal coming to Rawdon," Hannah said. "I got the news from John Harder, but it's all over town now."

Mulvane nodded. "I got it from Bagley," he said. "I hear the nesters are behind it."

"What can you do?" Hannah asked.

Mulvane shrugged. "Can't stop them from leaving the grove now," he said, "but I can give them a rough time once they're settled on their claims."

Hannah nodded and frowned. "There's something else," she said. "Mr. Quill was out near the Rocking Chair ranch again, yesterday."

Mulvane looked at her. "You saw him?" he asked.

"Not with Ward," Hannah admitted, "but he was coming from the direction of the Whiting place where they'd met before."

"You're pretty sure they're in this together?" Mulvane murmured.

"Quite sure," Hannah said, "but I can't prove anything."

"I think he has a killer on my trail, too," Mulvane growled, "but I can't prove that, either."

He did wonder, though, what the delay was. If Quill and Bryant were cooking up a deal whereby the emigrants would buy out Rocking Chair, they were certainly taking their time about it, and while they were wasting time the hired gun of the Cattleman's Association could be putting on more and more pressure, forcing them possibly even to leave the grove. Bryant should have known that, if Quill didn't.

Hannah was saying slowly, "I almost look upon Ward as a nester, himself. I suppose if he's dealing with them, and selling out to them, he is one of them in a way, and maybe even worse. What do you think, Mr. Mulvane?"

Mulvane looked down at the worn carpet in the hotel lobby, and he wondered what she was driving at by putting Bryant in the same category as the nesters.

"I've been thinking," Hannah went on, "that we should take this up with Harder and the other cattlemen before it's too late."

"Bryant could deny everything," Mulvane told her, "and then after he'd sold Rocking Chair he could move out without any trouble."

He couldn't imagine a man like Ward Bryant, however, running from the likes of John Harder and Ad Baisley. It was more like Bryant to tell them all to go to hell after he'd made his deal, and then ride off at his leisure with his profits.

"Not much you can tell Harder," Mulvane went on. "All you have to go on is that you've seen them together several times, and that doesn't prove that they're cooking up a deal."

"Then why are they meeting?" Hannah demanded, "and in secret."

Mulvane rubbed his hands together. He still hadn't figured out, himself, how a man like Ward Bryant had gotten mixed up with the little easterner who'd brought emigrants out to Rawdon.

"If Ward sells out," Hannah was saying, "we're all ruined in this part of the country, especially with this marshal coming in now to enforce the law."

As Mulvane pondered the problem he saw Ruby Watkins coming down the stairs from the upper floor where she'd evidently been cleaning. She looked at the two of them sitting in a corner of the lobby, and there was a definite frown on her face.

Hannah said slowly, "If I lose Box C I'm finished," and then impulsively she put her hand on Mulvane's hand, and she added, "Please help me to keep it."

"Reckon I'm being paid to help you keep it," Mulvane reminded her, and he wondered what more she expected him to do.

"I'm worried about Ward, now, more than about the nesters," Hannah told him.

"Reckon I could go out and put a bullet through him," Mulvane said with forced humor, and then he looked up, and he was shocked to see an expression almost of eagerness deep down in the girl's beautiful blue eyes.

She was looking at him steadily, and Mulvane stared back at her, the shock still in him. He realized that he must have been mistaken because Hannah Carrington was smiling at him, and she said softly, "Please, Mr. Mulvane, this is not a joking matter."

That eager look had gone out of her eyes now, and Mulvane was not even sure that he'd seen it there, but when Hannah left him minutes later, going to her room, and he was able to consider the matter more rationally, and to put the various pieces of this puzzle together. He began to wonder just what Hannah *did* want him to do.

She'd told him that she suspected Ward Bryant, and she'd asked him to keep an eye on Ward, which meant exactly nothing. If Bryant were guilty of double-dealing the only way to stop him was to get rid of him. Hannah hadn't said that, but was that what she meant?

Still shaken, Mulvane stepped out of the hotel and into the Cheyenne Saloon, knowing that he needed a stiff drink. He stood up at the bar, nursing the drink, and staring into the bar mirror. If Hannah Carrington wanted Ward Bryant out of the way she'd come to the right man, and she knew it. Mulvane wondered if this were the reason she had suddenly changed her attitude toward him. She'd been unfriendly when he'd first met her in the lodge hall, but now she was overly friendly, even soliciting his help.

He tried to shake these evil thoughts from his mind, but it was very difficult. He was beginning to wonder if there wasn't something substantially wrong with the Box C ranch woman. She was too beautiful, too poised, too cool, and too friendly with a hired gun; she should have regarded him with contempt.

He wondered if there was any way in which he could verify her story that Bryant and Quill were working together. Then he thought of Quill, the fat man with the pig's eyes, and the soft hands, and the round, pumpkin head—an easterner. He was undoubtedly a thieving, unscrupulous agent out to make money from the poor nesters, but he did not have that hardness characteristic of men like Ward Bryant. Very possibly, he could be made to crack.

The more Mulvane thought about Quill, the more he became convinced that Quill was his man. Standing at the Cheyenne bar he almost had to laugh considering the peculiarities of this situation. Always before it had been a simple fight between the ranchers and the nesters, and the ranchers had always won because they'd had Mulvane and his big, easy gun on their side. Now, here in Rawdon, it was different. Apparently one of the ranchers had defaulted to the side of the nesters, and a beautiful girl—whom Mulvane supposed was Bryant's fiance—had asked the hired gun to spy upon her man, and if his senses were not betraying him, it almost appeared as if Miss Carrington wanted Bryant out of the way for good.

Mulvane looked at the clock on the wall on the other side of the bar, noting that it was nearly ten o'clock in the morning. The bar room was empty, and a swamper was pushing the sawdust around with a broom, the chairs up on the tables as he worked.

Paying for his drink, Mulvane left the Cheyenne, walking back to the hotel, and then down the alley to the stables at the rear. He saddled the claybank, and then took a stub of pencil and a scrap of paper from his pocket and wrote a brief note.

It was addressed to Arno Quill, instructing Quill to meet him at noon at the old Whiting place. He signed the note with a "B" rather than Bryant's full name.

Mulvane did not think that Quill would recognize Bryant's handwriting, but he printed the letters of the note anyway, finishing with the big "B."

Then he looked about for the wizened little hostler who had been taking care of the claybank at the hotel stables. Finding the man at the rear of the stables, pitching hay to one of the horses, he said to him easily, "Like to make two dollars pretty quick?"

The old man grinned at him, revealing toothless gums. "Do a hell of a lot for two dollars," he said.

Mulvane took two silver dollars from his pocket and flipped one of them up into the air. He said, "Five minutes work, and all you have to do is keep your mouth shut."

"Reckon I'm listenin', mister," the hostler chuckled.

"Take this note to Mr. Quill's room," Mulvane told him. "You know Quill?"

"Know the sidewinder," the hostler nodded.

Mulvane handed him the folded note. "Take this to his room in the hotel. Give it to him and get out. If he wants to know who gave you the note, tell him you don't know the man. You got that?"

"Got it," the hostler nodded, and he was looking at the two gleaming silver dollars in Mulvane's hand.

"One dollar now," Mulvane told him. "The other when you get back."

The hostler snatched at the note and the coin, and disappeared through the stable door. He was back in a matter of minutes, grinning, holding out his hand for the other dollar.

"He say anything?" Mulvane asked.

"Never had no chance," the hostler grinned. "Knocked on his door, an' when he opened it, I handed him the note, an' left."

Mulvane flipped the coin to him. "He might

come in here and ask you where you got the note," he said. "Remember what to tell him."

"Don't know the man," the hostler grinned, "an' it wasn't you. That how you want it, Mr. Mulvane?"

Mulvane smiled at him. He looked at the old man, thoughtfully, for a moment, and then he said, "You see me work on Jud Faraday last night?"

The old man nodded, his eyes narrowed.

"You tell Quill where you got that note, and you'll be Faraday the next time."

"I ain't tellin' him," the hostler grinned. "I ain't a damned fool."

Mulvane stepped into the saddle, and then rode out of the alley, and into the street. He rode west, heading for the trace out to Rocking Chair, and as he rode past Sheriff Bagley's office in town, he noticed that the blind was down. He noticed, also, that the shade moved slightly as he went past, and he was confident that Ed Bagley had watched him go by as he watched everything else in this town.

The day was warm as Mulvane rode along, and in a few minutes he unbuttoned his jacket and folded it, placing it on the saddle behind him. White, fleecy clouds sailed overhead, and the breeze came from the northwest, from a string of ragged mountains, forming the outermost limits of this rich grazing land.

He rode on, passing several of the ranches before reaching Rocking Chair, and this time he gave the bunkhouse a wide berth moving around it to the north, and then keeping on in this direction. The old Whiting place was supposed to be on the north range according to Hannah Carrington, and he had no doubt that he would run across it without too much difficulty.

He passed clumps of Rocking Chair stock grazing on the slopes, and he kept riding until he saw in the distance a scraggly line of willows which always meant water. The Whiting place would be somewhere along this stream.

He followed the water north and east about a half mile coming upon the abandoned ranch-house very suddenly around the bend in the stream. There was not much of it left. This had been quite an expansive ranchhouse at one time, but it had fallen upon evil days.

The house was rectangular in shape, low, squat, the chimney fallen down, and part of the porch roof caved in. All of the windows were smashed in, and the door fallen from its hinges.

A wagon shed stood a short distance behind the house, and Mulvane turned the claybank in that direction. He tied the horse under the shed, and then he rolled a cigarette, and smoked it through, squatting on his heels in the warm sunshine outside the shed.

After awhile he walked back to the shade of the

willows along the creek where he could have a better look at the approach from the south. He sat on a rock and tossed little pebbles into the water while he waited, still not sure whether Arno Quill would turn up at the Whiting house or not.

If Quill had met Bryant here before, he would come again. If he had not, he would know nothing about the Whiting house, nor would he even understand who had signed the note. This, then, was a test of Hannah Carrington, also.

Walking out to the fringe of willows he looked out across the hills, seeing nothing as yet, but the hour was still early. Over to the east he saw a dust cloud where some riders were moving a band of stock. They were too far away to be seen, however.

To the south he saw a thin column of smoke which probably came from Rocking Chair ranch-house. The sardonic thought struck him that, perhaps, Bryant, also, was riding this way, having arranged a real meeting with Arno Quill.

He went back to have another look at the claybank, and then took the animal down to the creek to water it. Walking back with the horse to the shed he passed within fifteen or twenty yards of the house, and as he did so, he was positive that he'd seen a faint movement near one of the windows.

He kept walking, letting the claybank move up ahead of him so that the horse was between himself and the watcher in the house, but he still held his breath as he walked, and he was glad when he'd reached the safety of the shed.

Someone was in the Whiting house. He hadn't heard a horse come up, nor had he seen an animal in the vicinity, but someone was there, and for a purpose. If the man in the house was there to bushwhack him, he could have done it any time within the past half-hour as Mulvane had been out in the open many times. Either that, or he had just arrived, slipping into the house on the other side, and was now waiting for a clean shot at him.

Mulvane stood in the shed next to the claybank, concealed from the house by the far wall of the shed, and he stood there for several long moments before making his move. Looking through some of the cracks in the rear wall of the shed he could see the line of willows and the creek winding toward the east. Through another crack in the side wall he could see the Whiting house. There was one window at the rear, and Mulvane had no doubt that his man was watching the shed now from that window.

He had a look around the corner of the shed where he was standing, and then he tested some of the boards, finding one which was fairly loose. He put his weight against the board, pushing firmly until he could get his fingers on it. As he pushed it back away from the frame he slid the muzzle of his gun into the crevice, working quietly, gently, not wanting the man inside the house to know what was going on.

Several rusted nails held the board, but he worked on them slowly, applying more and more pressure, using the barrel of the gun as a wedge and a lever. Then he grasped the board firmly with both hands and pushed back, loosening it from the frame. He had an opening in the rear of the shed now of eight or nine inches in width through which he could easily squeeze his body.

Gun in hand, then, he slipped through the crevice, coming out on the rear of the shed. The shed was now between himself and the Whiting house, and by crouching low he could make his way down to the creek without being seen from the house.

It was about fifteen yards to the willows, and Mulvane made it without any trouble. Standing under the trees he planned his next move. He was sure the man in the house was not Arno Quill. The easterner could not have gotten here so quickly, although there was the possibility that he'd learned who had sent the note, and had sent someone else.

Moving up the creek, keeping concealed among the willows, Mulvane went about a hundred yards above the house, and then he circled behind a low ridge, coming up on the west side of the house. He had to cross a distance of about twenty yards between the ridge and the house, and he was clearly in the open as he made his run for the wall.

If the man inside was aware of the fact that Mulvane had slipped out of the wagon shed, and was now coming up on the other side of the building, he would have a rifle trained on him at this moment, but Mulvane had to take the long risk.

Pulling his hat down firmly on his head, he ran swiftly and lightly across the open space, almost holding his breath as he waited for that bullet, but it never came. In another moment he sank down in the shade against the wall of the house.

He crouched here for several moments, listening carefully, before going on. He had not been seen, and the advantage now was reversed. He moved slowly, lifting himself from the ground and stepping toward the nearest window.

Standing upright he could look into the house. He did not wish to risk going up on the rickety porch. The window was his best bet. Reaching for the window sill, he lifted himself up, making no noise as he climbed into the room.

Even as he did so, he saw the wet sand on the wooden floor as he stepped down, and he smiled faintly, knowing that the man at the other end of the house had entered through this same window, coming from the direction of the creek where he'd picked up this sand on his boot.

Gun in hand, Mulvane waited again, and then

he took one tentative step forward, hoping that the boards wouldn't squeak. He took another step, and then another toward the doorway which opened into a kind of hall with other rooms leading from it.

Reaching the entrance way he waited again, listening before going out into the corridor. He had the hammer of the Colt .44 in readiness as he stepped out into the hall.

Very distinctly, he smelled cigarette smoke in the house, the final proof that a man was here, waiting for him. He had rolled a cigarette, and was smoking it now, taking his time, waiting for Mulvane to come out of the wagon shed.

Mulvane stood in the hall, trying to figure the layout of this house. The room with the window at the rear was probably at the far end of this little corridor, a distance of about eight or ten feet.

He was about to take a step toward that room when he heard a faint, tinkling sound, and he knew, then, who the man was in the other room. That sound had come from a jangling spur. The man who'd brought him the death message in the Great Western Saloon had worn spurs which jangled just like this when he walked. He had no doubt, also, that this same man, for a price, had waited in his hotel room, and then shot Jud Faraday by mistake. He was coming now very close to the end of his rope.

Chapter 8

Mulvane took one slow step after the other, moving noiselessly down the hallway. The boards were fairly solid, giving no sound. He took two steps, then three, and then he was very close to the door, gun in hand, the hammer drawn back.

He could hear a faint sound in the room as if a man had moved his weight, and as he approached, he smelled the tobacco smoke more strongly.

In making his wide sweep around the Whiting house, Mulvane had almost forgotten completely about Arno Quill, who could at this moment be nearing the Whiting house.

As Mulvane was about to take that last step which would bring him up to the open doorway he heard Quill out in front of the house calling softly, "Bryant? Ward Bryant?"

The man in the back room made a break for the door as if he would look out the front window, and he came into the doorway not more than three feet from where Mulvane stood, his gun trained on him.

The man who had been laying in wait for him here, ready to put a bullet through him, was the rat-faced little messenger with the big Mexican spurs, and the twisted mouth. He had a gun in his right hand, but the muzzle of the gun was toward the floor as he appeared in the doorway.

Mulvane said gently, "Drop it, mister."

He had his Colt lined on the target, and it was impossible to miss. He saw the shock and the surprise come into the beady black eyes of the killer.

"Drop the gun," Mulvane snapped.

He wanted this man alive to find out who had sent him, but even as he gave the order he realized that he was not going to take him alive. He could see it in his eyes which were contracting, seeming to change color as he stared at Mulvane, making no sounds.

He made his move with the quickness of the animal which he resembled. With his free hand he slashed at Mulvane's gun hand, trying to push the gun toward the floor, and at the same time raise his own weapon.

At this close distance Mulvane had anticipated some kind of move, and he was ready when it came. Pulling back his own gun hand as the small man tried to grab it, he slashed down with the Colt across the killer's skull, knocking him back into the room.

He stepped in after the man, thinking he would find him only half conscious, but the rat-faced man had taken the gun barrel on the side of the head, and he was still very much in action. His gun was in his hand, and he was lifting the barrel when Mulvane fired, shooting down at him the way a man would shoot down at a deadly snake about to strike.

His bullet caught the small man squarely between the eyes, knocking his head back so that his hat fell from his head. He lay on the floor, arms outstretched, staring up at the ceiling with his dead eyes.

Immediately after, Mulvane heard a horse moving away from the house, and he ran back to the front to look out one of the windows. He had a brief glimpse of a rider on a chestnut horse, going across the creek, heading back in the direction of Rawdon. He recognized the short, fat Arno Quill without any difficulty. Quill had ridden out here to meet with Ward Bryant, proving Hannah Carrington's accusations that Bryant had been conniving with Quill.

Mulvane watched from the window until Quill had disappeared. Quill had not seen him, nor his horse, and he would ride back to Rawdon not knowing who had arranged to meet him at the Whiting house. Now, both he and Bryant would be on their guard, knowing that someone apparently knew what they were up to.

Going back to the rear room, Mulvane had his look at the dead man, and then reluctantly searched through his pockets for some kind of identification. He found some greasy greenbacks, some coins, a tobacco pouch, a bronze medallion which had brought him no luck whatever this day, and that was all.

A man of this caliber did not carry papers with him, and Mulvane had his doubts whether he would find anything on the dead man's saddle which must have been tied up along the creek.

Leaving the house, Mulvane walked down to the wagon shed, stepped into the saddle, and rode up along the creek until he located the horse, a small blue roan which carried the Pine Tree brand—a brand Mulvane had not seen in this part of the country.

He untied the horse, letting him run, knowing that sooner or later the animal would be picked up on the range and brought in to town. The shots had attracted no attention out here on the open range.

Riding back to Rawdon he entered town at about three o'clock in the afternoon. He paused first at Sheriff Bagley's office, dismounting there, and he was stepping into the office, when he saw Bagley hastening toward him from the direction of the Cheyenne Saloon.

Bagley was wiping his mouth with the back of his hand as if he'd just finished a drink, and he came up on the walk hurriedly, the excitement in his face, and he blurted out before Mulvane could say anything.

"U.S. marshal's in town, Mulvane. Just came in on the afternoon train. He's over at the Cheyenne now."

"What do you want me to do?" Mulvane asked him tersely, "shake hands with him?"

Bagley grinned. "Figured you'd like to know," he said.

"Something you ought to know," Mulvane told him. "There's a dead man out at the Whiting place, north range of Rocking Chair."

Bagley stared. "A dead man?" he repeated. "Who?"

"Ask him," Mulvane shrugged, and he walked down toward the hotel. He had to pass opposite the Cheyenne Saloon as he went to the hotel, and as he did so, he saw a man come out to look at him.

The man was tall, very slender, with a thin, hatchet face. He was dressed in black, and he wore a black, flat-crowned hat. The gun on his hip was worn very low, and his boots were polished and waxed. He wore a white shirt, and a black string tie, and his hair seemed to be black and long at the neck.

Mulvane had his leisurely look at the man, knowing him for the new marshal who had just arrived. Staring at him, though, the thought was running through Mulvane's mind that the new marshal could easily be another killer. He looked the part of a hired gun!

Moving on into the hotel, Mulvane stepped into the dining room for a late lunch. Ruby Watkins hurried out of the kitchen to wait on him, her eyes lighting up with pleasure when she saw him.

"I'm glad you're back," Ruby told him. "I had a feeling this morning that you were in trouble."

Mulvane smiled. "No trouble I couldn't handle," he assured her. He changed the subject, and he said, "Your uncle been back?"

"He hasn't bothered me," Ruby admitted. "I hope he never comes into town again."

Mulvane had his lunch, and when he'd finished he sat at the table smoking a cigar through, and as he smoked he found himself thinking about the new marshal. He'd seen gunmen before, and this tall, slim man in black had all the earmarks of the trade.

Ruby said, "Will you have more coffee, Mr. Mulvane?"

Mulvane shook his head. He said, "Miss Carrington still at the hotel?"

"I haven't noticed," Ruby frowned.

Looking out the window, Mulvane saw Hannah coming down the street with a package under her arm. She'd evidently just stepped out of one of the stores.

Mulvane got up and moved toward the lobby. He was on the porch when Hannah reached the hotel. She smiled at him, nodding her head in greeting. As she came up on the porch she said, "I suppose you've heard that the new marshal is in town."

"Saw him," he said, "and I don't like the looks of him."

He looked down at Hannah knowing that he'd made a mistake in doubting her. She'd spoken the truth when she'd said that Quill and Bryant were having meetings.

He didn't tell her, though, about his ride out to the Whiting place, nor of the message he'd had sent to Arno Quill.

"If the marshal accompanies the nester wagons out of the grove," Hannah said, "there's not much you can do, is there?"

Mulvane shook his head. "Reckon they can get out on the ranges," he stated, "but they might not be able to stay there."

They were standing on the porch when Mulvane saw Quill and the new marshal coming toward them. Quill's round, fleshy face was triumphant. As he came up he nodded toward Mulvane and he said to the marshal, "There's your man, Rudabaugh."

Mulvane had a better look at the marshal from close up. He had intense black eyes, a thin, white face, and a narrow, pointed chin.

Rudabaugh said softly, "You're Mulvane?"

Mulvane nodded.

"Heard about you," Rudabaugh smiled, "in plenty of places, mister."

"Reckon I've been in plenty of places," Mulvane told him.

"He's put the fear in these poor farmers out in the grove," Quill was saying excitedly. "Not a one of them will leave the grove because they're afraid they'll be shot."

Rudabaugh said gently, "They'll leave in the morning, Mr. Quill, and there's nothing Mr. Mulvane will do about it."

Mulvane looked down at the gun on Rudabaugh's right hip. The holster was black, smooth, oily, and the gun was a Smith & Wesson .44. He had the queer feeling that he'd seen this man before somewhere, years ago, not under the name of Rudabaugh, but another name, and another position in life. This man may have been a marshal now, but at one time he had been a killer.

Rudabaugh was saying, "We do not expect any trouble tomorrow, Mulvane, or any time, and if there is trouble you will answer to me."

Mulvane smiled at him. "Will I?" he said softly.

"You will," Rudabaugh nodded.

Quill said, "You try to fight the United States Government, Mulvane, and you'll have the county swarming with troopers. They'll run you down like a rat."

"We'll see," Mulvane said.

Rudabaugh said, "You'll know me the next time, mister."

Quite suddenly Mulvane knew him, *then*. He'd met this man eight or ten years ago, when he'd gone by the name of Ballister. Although quite young, Ballister had had a reputation with a gun, and a string of killings behind him. Mulvane had been unknown at that time, and Ballister had taken no particular notice of him, and did not recognize him now.

Ballister could have reformed now, and become a U.S. marshal, but Mulvane doubted it very much. It was more likely that Rudabaugh had been brought in by Bryant and Quill for the same purpose that they had brought in the other two hired killers.

Mulvane watched the two of them crossing the street, heading toward Sheriff Bagley's office, and he wondered if he ought to confide at this time in Hannah Carrington, who was still standing on the porch, and who had been listening to the conversation. He decided that the less Hannah or anyone else knew, the better off he was.

"Reckon they've played their top card now," Mulvane murmured, "and they can't go any higher than that."

"Will you try to stop them?" Hannah asked.

Mulvane shook his head. "Reckon I'll know in the morning," he said.

He wondered if it would mean anything to her if he did stand up to Rudabaugh and was shot down.

Hannah was saying, "You think possibly Ward had anything to do with bringing this man here if he's in with Quill?"

"He must know about it," Mulvane told her.

"Then he's as guilty as Quill," Hannah murmured.

Mulvane didn't say anything to that. He could not dispute the logic of it, however.

Late that afternoon John Harder, Ad Baisley, and several other ranchers came into Rawdon, and stepped into Mulvane's room at the hotel. Mulvane had been half-expecting them, knowing that they would be worried.

Harder said glumly as he sat on the edge of a chair in the room, "What in hell do we do now, Mulvane?"

"If he really is a United States marshal," Mulvane said, "reckon there's not too much we can do."

Harder frowned and stared at him. "What do you mean—*if* he's a United States marshal?" he asked.

Mulvane shrugged. He put a cigar in his mouth and touched a light to it. "Who has the power in this territory to bring in a government official?" he asked.

The short gray-haired man looked at him and

then at the other men in the room. Harder said slowly, "Reckon that would be Ed Bagley."

Mulvane smiled. "You figure Bagley brought him in, then?"

"If he did," one of the other men grated, "Ed's askin' for a hell of a lot o' trouble."

Harder said to Mulvane, "You don't figure this Rudabaugh is really a United States marshal?"

Mulvane shrugged. "Have to find that out," he said. "Reckon the man you ought to talk to is Ed Bagley."

Harder said to one of the other men, "Get Bagley to hell over here."

They sat in Mulvane's room, smoking, saying very little, waiting for Bagley to come up. In a few minutes they heard voices on the stairs, and then Bagley came through the door with the rancher who had gone for him. He was smiling as he came in, and he said, "Looks like a regular meeting, boys."

Mulvane closed the door, and then leaned against the wall, arms folded, the cigar in his mouth.

John Harder snapped, "What the hell you know about this man, Rudabaugh?"

Bagley looked at him, and at the other men in the room. "Rudabaugh?" he repeated. "U.S. marshal? Reckon I'm not followin' you boys."

"Who brought him in here?" Harder demanded. "You know anything about it, Bagley?"

The sheriff of Rawdon stared at him. "It's that damned Quill. He's behind it," he said. "That's why he's been holdin' things up so long. He was waitin' for this chap to show up. Reckon he's got connections back in Washington."

Mulvane said from the wall, "You see his credentials, Bagley?"

Ed Bagley turned to look at him. "You don't figure he's really a marshal?" he asked.

"You see his papers?" Mulvane repeated.

"First thing I asked to see," Bagley said, "when Quill brought him around."

Mulvane noticed that there was a very slight hesitation before he spoke. He didn't know whether Harder or the others had noticed it, but he had been watching carefully for it.

John Harder said glumly, "Reckon that's it, boys. This man's here. Quill got him here some way, and that's the end of it. We fight him, and we'll have the whole United States Government on our backs."

Bagley said quickly, "He's askin' me to back up his play around here. Figured I'd kind of be in some other place when trouble began."

Mulvane said from the wall, "You can go some other place now, Bagley," and he saw the hatred come into Bagley's small, amber eyes. In another moment, however, the sheriff was smiling at him complacently, and he said as he walked toward the door, "My hand's in with you boys. Reckon you know that."

Harder said grimly, "It had damn well better be, Ed."

When Bagley left Harder said to Mulvane, "Reckon you have your answer, mister."

"Do I?" Mulvane smiled. "I met this Rudabaugh years ago. He was a killer, and a hired gun hand, then. If he's a U.S. marshal now he's changed damn quick."

Harder said, "Bagley saw his credentials."

"Bagley's a damned liar," Mulvane said. "Reckon you boys know that. The papers could have been forged even if Bagley was telling the truth. Best way for you to find out about Ruda-baugh is to send a wire to Washington. They'll let you know pretty quick whether they have a man in this town by the name of Rudabaugh."

Harder nodded slowly. "Don't know how this man Quill could get a marshal down here without going through Ed Bagley. Maybe he did, and maybe he didn't. We ought to find out. We'll get that wire off right away, Mulvane."

Mulvane nodded. He watched them file out of the room, and after they were gone he went down for his supper.

Ruby Watkins as usual waited on him. She said as she brought him his coffee later, "There's going to be trouble now, isn't there with this marshal in town?"

120

"Could be," Mulvane nodded.

"I wish you'd go away from here," Ruby told him, "before you're killed."

Mulvane just smiled at her. "Everybody dies," he said.

"You don't have to die here," Ruby said. "Go away!"

"I'm paid to stay here," Mulvane reminded her. "I'm not running out now."

He was having his second cup of coffee when John Harder came back to the hotel alone, his face grim. He handed Mulvane a yellow slip of paper, and Mulvane read it casually. The telegram stated that the Department of Justice had no knowledge of a man by the name of Rudabaugh, nor had they dispatched a United States marshal to the town of Rawdon.

"Wait'll I see that damned Bagley," Harder grated.

Mulvane struck a match, touched it to the edge of the telegram, lighting it, and then he dropped the slip of paper into a plate, watching it burn up.

"Reckon I wouldn't tell Bagley anything if I were you, Harder," he said.

The rancher stared at him. "You don't figure Bagley's double-crossing us?" he asked slowly.

Mulvane shrugged. "Is Bagley an honest man?" he countered. "Reckon you boys don't want an honest man wearing that badge, do you, Harder?"

"All right," Harder snapped, his face reddening.

"We're in this thing up to our necks. Some of us have been running stock on this range for the past forty years. We're not being run off by a pack of damned farmers, even though the government says they have a right to come in here and settle. We're the ones who fought for it, Mulvane."

Mulvane nodded, remembering how his father had talked along the same lines, but it hadn't done any good.

"I'm here," Mulvane reminded him, "to see that they don't take over your range."

Harder looked a little mollified. "How do you figure on handling this Rudabaugh?" he asked.

"I'll handle him," Mulvane said. "That's my job."

He watched the telegram burn down to a black crisp, and then he said to Harder, "I wouldn't tell anybody about this wire, not even any of the other ranchers."

Harder was looking at him. "You're going to call Rudabaugh?" he said slowly.

Mulvane nodded. "He's asked for it."

He wondered as he said it, though, if he, Mulvane, were not asking for it, himself. Rudabaugh was not Ed Bagley, nor even Ward Bryant. Rudabaugh was the cold professional, fast and cool on the draw, and as deadly as a rattler. He killed for cash, and he was not afraid to die, and he had his pride like a bright banner always waving above his head. A man like this did not have too much for which to live, and thus he had that little edge on other men who did. Mulvane was well aware of this fact because it had kept him alive the past eight or ten years.

Chapter 9

That evening the nesters came in to celebrate, having heard from Quill that in the morning they would be pulling out of the grove, protected by a U.S. marshal.

Mulvane watched from the porch of the hotel, seeing crowds of them walking in from the grove, and listening to their talk. He was convinced in his own mind now that Sheriff Bagley was in with Quill and Ward Bryant, but he still did not understand why, if Bryant were planning on selling Rocking Chair he did not do so immediately, unless it was that the nesters were afraid to take over the range without a government official behind them. It meant that Bagley and Bryant were double-crossing the Cattleman's Association.

He noticed that Harder and the others were staying in town tonight because they wanted to be on hand for the fireworks in the morning. Hannah Carrington was still at the hotel, also, and as Mulvane sat in his chair on the porch, she came out and stood near him. Then she said, "They're pretty sure they're going into the Promised Land, aren't they?"

"They're sure," Mulvane nodded, "but they won't go."

"Then you're going to fight him?"

Mulvane didn't say anything. Sitting in the shadows he saw Rudabaugh and Arno Quill come out of the Great Western, and head down the street to the Cheyenne Saloon. Quill apparently was in high spirits, stopping now and then to speak with groups of nesters on the street, and then moving on again.

Rudabaugh walked along with him, taking no part in the conversations, and Mulvane knew that this man undoubtedly felt the same contempt for the farmers as he did, himself, but Rudabaugh's gun was on the side of the nesters, and he would kill for them as quickly as he would kill for anyone else.

"I don't know how you can stop them now," Hannah was saying.

"Reckon we'll know more about it in the morning," Mulvane told her.

Harder, who had taken a room at the hotel, came out, and seeing Mulvane on the porch, he paused, nodding his greeting to Hannah, and he said, "You figure you'll be needing any of our boys tomorrow, Mulvane?"

"Keep them out of the way," Mulvane answered, "unless you want a pitched battle with plenty of people dead."

"It'll just be Rudabaugh and you, then," Harder said slowly.

"Better that way," Mulvane nodded.

Hannah said, "If you kill a government man, they'll hang you for it, Mr. Mulvane."

"I don't figure they will," Mulvane said, and he gave her no more information. Then he reached into his shirt pocket and took out a slip of paper, handing it to Harder. He said, "Reckon you'd better keep this until tomorrow evening, Mr. Harder."

"What is it?" Harder asked. It was too dark to see, but Mulvane had given him the check the Cattleman's Association had given him.

Mulvane said, "Won't do me any good if I'm not around tomorrow night, and I won't have earned it."

"You got a right to it," Harder protested. "Reckon that's how we hired you, Mulvane."

"If Rudabaugh knocks me down tomorrow morning," Mulvane smiled, "you've hired a bag of wind. Those nesters will be all over your range the day after, and you know it."

Hannah said, "I wish it could be settled without guns."

"You know it can't be," Mulvane told her. "Never has been."

In many ways he couldn't understand this girl. She'd told him when they first met that she didn't want any killings, yet she'd tried to set him on

Ward Bryant, and she must have known that with Bryant it would have come to guns.

The three of them stood on the porch for some time, and then Harder said in a gruff attempt at friendliness, "Buy you a drink, Mulvane."

Mulvane stepped into the Cheyenne Saloon with him. He had his drink, played a few hands of poker at one of the tables, and then retired early. He'd seen no more of Rudabaugh that night, and he wondered how the killer slept before a morning like this.

In the morning he had a light breakfast in the dining room, and he was still sitting in the room when Quill and Rudabaugh came in. Rudabaugh was not staying at the hotel, as far as Mulvane knew, but the best food in town was served here, and it was not unusual for him to be coming in.

As the two men passed the table where Mulvane was sitting, Rudabaugh said softly, "See you at the grove, Mr. Mulvane?"

Mulvane smiled at him. "You might," he said, and he let it rest that way.

When Ruby waited on his table, she said, "There's going to be a gunfight, isn't there, Mr. Mulvane?"

"If there's a gunfight," he told her, "you'll hear about it one way or the other."

"That marshal's going to take the nesters out of the grove," Ruby said slowly, "and you can't stop them."

Mulvane said, "He aims to take them out."

"And you can't stop them," Ruby repeated.

Mulvane just smiled. After eating, he paid his bill and went out. As he passed Ruby near the door, she watched him go, white-faced. She whispered, "Please don't get in trouble."

Mulvane frowned. "I figure on coming back," he said.

He went out to the stable and saddled the claybank, and then he rode out of the alley into the street. When he reached the far end of town he saw the ranchers waiting for him. There were about twenty-five men in the group, and he noticed that Ward Bryant was with them now. Harder had promised that there wouldn't be a pitched battle of any kind, but he was there to see that the nesters didn't try to aid the marshal in this fight.

The rumor had gone out that there was to be a showdown this morning, and the ranchers had all ridden in, bringing with them some of their riders.

Bryant sat astride his bay horse, a cold smile on his face, and as Mulvane drew near he said, "Hear you figure on tackling the United States Government this morning, Mulvane."

"That could be," Mulvane nodded. "You in on it, Bryant?"

Bryant shook his head and grinned. "Not this deal," he said.

Mulvane rode on past the group, heading out toward the grove. When he reached the grove he saw the wagons being loaded, and horses being put into the traces. The grove was a beehive of activity.

The nesters had been camped here for several weeks now, and they'd erected tarpaulin tents attached to their wagons, but everything was coming down now, and being loaded back into the wagons, ready for moving.

Mulvane rode up to within about twenty-five yards of the grove, and then he stopped. He sat astride the claybank, watching, as he rolled a cigarette.

The ranchers and their riders had trailed out after him, and when the emigrants saw them coming on, they stopped to watch, coming out to the edge of the grove.

Mulvane was alone, apart from the ranchers, smoking his cigarette now, and as he sat there he saw Joab Watkins striding out of the grove, walking straight toward him, his lean, thin figure bent forward as he came.

Watkins said triumphantly, "Can't stop us now, Mulvane. We got a U.S. marshal out here to see that you don't."

Mulvane just nodded at him, and kept on smoking.

"You can take that whole crowd of tinhorns with you, too," Watkins yelled. "They start any trouble out here, an' we'll have the government after 'em now."

Again, Mulvane nodded, saying nothing.

"I'll be gettin' my girl back, too," Watkins grated. "You see if I don't, mister."

"You had your say?" Mulvane asked him finally.

Joab went back to the grove, and in a few moments Mulvane saw a man riding out of the grove, heading back toward town, undoubtedly to tell Quill and Rudabaugh of this new development.

Mulvane sat astride the claybank, his face expressionless, waiting patiently. Many of the nesters were standing at the edge of the grove, now, just looking at him, saying nothing. They saw him, and they saw the ranchers behind him with big guns on their hips, and they were worried now.

A woman walked out a little beyond the others, and began to berate Mulvane, but after awhile her husband came out to pull her back under the trees.

Then Mulvane heard a low murmur come up from the crowd, and turning his head slightly, he saw three riders coming up fast. He recognized Ed Bagley's chestnut mare, and then he saw Rudabaugh astride a buckskin. The third man was Arno Quill.

Rudabaugh was up ahead of the other two, tall

and thin in the saddle, riding loosely, where Quill bounced as he came on. The three of them passed the waiting ranchers, and approached Mulvane. As they drew up closer, Mulvane saw the worry in Bagley's eyes. Quill, also, was grim, but determined as he rode up, and he snapped, "What the hell is the meaning of this, Mulvane? You're not going to stop these wagons today."

Mulvane didn't even look at him. He was looking straight at Rudabaugh, who had pulled up his buckskin horse, and was sitting about fifteen feet away, a slow smile on his face.

"We got a United States marshal with us this morning," Quill almost screamed. "You'd better move off, Mulvane."

Mulvane still didn't look at him, but he said, "Who's the gentleman in black, Quill?"

"You know damned well who he is," Quill snapped. "What kind of a bluff is this?"

Mulvane said to Ed Bagley, "You know this man, Sheriff?"

Bagley blinked, swallowed, and then said uneasily, "Reckon he's a United States marshal."

"You've seen his credentials?" Mulvane asked. He was watching Rudabaugh all the time, noting the way he sat with his body very loose and relaxed, his right hand at his side, close to the butt of the gun on his hip.

Bagley hesitated, and Mulvane snapped at him, "You see his credentials, Bagley?"

"Saw them," Bagley muttered.

"You're a damned liar, too," Mulvane told him flatly. "This man is known as Ames Ballister from the Big Bend country, and he's a paid killer, and you paid to bring him here to kill me. That right, Quill?"

Arno Quill seemed stunned for a moment, and he had nothing to say. Rudabaugh spoke, then, for the first time. He spoke softly so that Mulvane could hardly hear him. He said, "You talk a lot, Mulvane."

"Like to show me your credentials?" Mulvane smiled.

"To hell with you and credentials," Rudabaugh chuckled. "We're past that, and you know it."

Mulvane said over his shoulder to Quill and Bagley, "Back off."

They both knew what he meant. Both men at this time were fairly close to him, and when lead started to fly there was a good possibility they would be hit.

Bagley moved first, getting his mare out of range quickly, and Quill moved off more slowly, and Mulvane heard him muttering to himself as he did so.

Rudabaugh said curiously, "You know me, Mulvane?" There was a faint touch of pride in his voice.

"Knew you years ago," Mulvane nodded. "You came to the wrong town this time, Ballister."

The thin man shrugged. "Who knows what's the wrong town," he said, "or the last town. Who knows that, Mulvane?"

Mulvane had no answer to that. He was ready now, as ready as he would ever be. The claybank was standing perfectly still as if realizing what was about to happen, and understanding his part.

Rudabaugh said casually, "Your friends backing up your play, Mulvane?"

Mulvane shook his head. "You know my job," he stated. "You know what I have to do. They'll keep out of it."

Rudabaugh nodded as if satisfied. Both men had come to the end of talk now, and they sat there, looking at each other, both cool, both very calm, their horses standing still.

In the grove the nesters watched fascinated, and even the children seemed to have stopped crying. Out on the open plain the ranchers sat and watched.

Mulvane said gently, "Better this way, Rudabaugh. Just the two of us."

Rudabaugh nodded.

"Draw your gun," Mulvane told him.

Rudabaugh's right hand moved, and Mulvane went with him. Both guns seemed to explode simultaneously. Mulvane's hat was pushed back on his head by a slug which came within an inch of tearing off the top of his skull. Rudabaugh fell backward from his saddle, his body hitting the ground, and he lay there in a heap without moving.

The buckskin he'd been riding nervously walked off. Mulvane dismounted, gun in hand, and he adjusted his hat as he walked up to the man on the ground. He noticed that Rudabaugh's gun had dropped from his hand as he fell, and was lying in the dust, and then he holstered his own gun and bent down to roll Rudabaugh over.

As he did so he could see that the man was still breathing. A cascade of blood flowed down over the right side of his face, and Mulvane could see where his bullet had grazed Rudabaugh's left temple, gouging the hair away just above the ear. Rudabaugh was very much alive, but knocked unconscious by the bullet from Mulvane's gun.

Bagley was striding over now, and Quill followed. John Harder and Ward Bryant came up, also, and they stood around, looking down at the man on the ground as Mulvane straightened up.

Mulvane said to Quill, "Get one of those nesters to take him in to town. He's not fighting any more today."

Quill looked at him, his face gray, and then he turned and strode off toward the grove. Ward Bryant said, "You're asking for trouble, Mulvane, shooting up a U.S. marshal."

Mulvane stepped into the saddle, drew his gun again and ejected the empty shell, sliding a fresh one into the cylinder. He said softly, "Did I shoot a marshal, Bryant?"

He rode off, then, heading back to town, and as he passed the ranchers there, he saw Hannah Carrington sitting astride her black mare. She'd been watching this fight, and he hadn't known she was there. Evidently, she'd ridden out after he'd reached the grove.

Hannah said as he came up, "You kill him?"

"Head wound," Mulvane shook his head. "Reckon he'll be around a while."

"Then there'll be more trouble," Hannah murmured.

Mulvane nodded. "We didn't settle too much today," he admitted.

He realized that with men like Rudabaugh you didn't settle anything short of death.

He rode on past Hannah Carrington, and into town, and as he came up to the hotel he saw Ruby Watkins waiting there on the porch. She'd heard the shots from the grove, and she'd been waiting to see if he would come back alive.

"You all right?" Ruby asked him slowly.

"You worried?" Mulvane smiled at her. He dismounted, tying the claybank out in front of the hotel.

"I'm glad he didn't kill you," Ruby whispered as he came up on the porch.

"He may the next time," Mulvane told her. "He's still alive, and nothing has been settled.

135

If he'd killed me it might have settled a lot."

As he sat down on the porch he saw some of the ranchers trickling back to town. Harder and Bryant stepped into the Cheyenne for a drink, Harder lifting a hand to Mulvane from across the street.

A while later a buckboard came into town with Rudabaugh sitting in the back of it, his head bandaged and bloody. He still looked dazed. The buckboard rolled down the street to a boarding-house where Rudabaugh had evidently taken a room.

Quill was with the wounded man, and he stared at Mulvane grimly as they went by, his hat pulled low on his head.

Ed Bagley rode in after the others, and as Mulvane had anticipated, the fat man, seeing him on the porch, came over, dismounted and tied his horse at the tie rack. He said as he came up on the porch, "Reckon you had me all wrong, Mulvane. This Rudabaugh showed me papers. What the hell was I supposed to do?"

Mulvane just looked at him as he rolled a cigarette. He had no words for this man. Bagley frowned and went on to the Cheyenne Saloon. He did say, though, before he left, that none of the nesters had left the grove since Rudabaugh had been shot.

Mulvane hadn't thought that they would. These farmers may have considered ganging up on him, alone, but they knew that he had the combined support of the ranchers and their riders behind him, not to mention the sheriff of Rawdon who they probably knew was a crook.

A doctor carrying a black bag hurried down to the boardinghouse where Rudabaugh had been taken, and was in the house for nearly half an hour before coming out.

Mulvane watched the man go by with his bag, and he thought of Rudabaugh lying there on the bed, his head bandaged, probably fully conscious now, and planning his revenge. Rudabaugh would never leave this town until Mulvane was dead, or he had been killed, himself. It was the nature of men of his caliber. Rudabaugh had his pride, and his pride had been trampled in the dust this morning in front of many people. A man of his profession could neither forgive nor forget. He could only retaliate, and this would be the single guiding motive of his life from this moment on.

Chapter 10

Later in the morning Mulvane saw Bryant and many of the others leaving town, riding back to their ranches. Bryant looked at him as he went past, and lifted a finger to him.

Hannah Carrington, also, went out to Box C, driving the buckboard, and an hour later, with the restlessness running through him, Mulvane rode the claybank out of town. He was tired of the ranchers, tired of the nesters, tired of men like Quill and Bagley, tired even of the cynical townspeople who watched and waited, taking no part in the fight, but still eager for blood.

It was good to get out into the open country again, with a clear sky overhead, and the smell of sage in his nostrils, and a good horse beneath him. He cut across open range, not wanting to meet anyone this afternoon. He wondered as he rode how soon Rudabaugh would be on his feet and looking for him with a gun.

The claybank followed the course of a little stream, pausing once to drink, and Mulvane sat in the saddle, very slack. After awhile the horse moved on again, Mulvane giving the animal almost a free rein as they followed the course of the stream, and then quite suddenly he knew where he was.

Inadvertently, coming in from the north this time, he had approached the old Whiting place again. He recognized the landmarks now, the surrounding hills, the slope leading down to the creek, and then in a few moments he saw the shingled roof, and the broken chimney of the house.

Late yesterday afternoon he'd seen Bagley dispatch the coroner's wagon out in the direction of the Whiting place to pick up the body of the man who had been killed. Strangely enough, Bagley had asked no more questions concerning the killing, apparently realizing that Mulvane had knocked over just another hired killer who had been sent out to destroy him.

He would have ridden on past the Whiting place, giving it a wide berth, but as he turned the claybank he saw a slight movement down among the trees in front of the house. When he stopped to look he could see a horse tied there.

The horse was a big bay, and he recognized it as Ward Bryant's. A second horse stood close by the first, a chestnut which could have belonged to anyone, but the third horse he recognized immediately as Hannah Carrington's black mare with the two white feet.

Hannah, Bryant, and a third party whom Mulvane did not know, were out here at the abandoned Whiting house. Pulling the claybank back among the trees where he could not be seen, Mulvane heard another rider approaching from the south, coming down the grade toward the creek, and then splashing across the water to dismount near the other three horses. This horse was a chestnut mare, and the man stepping out of the saddle was Ed Bagley.

Mulvane dismounted, also, a frown on his face, and he led the claybank up along the stream, tying the animal in under the trees where it could not be seen. Then he walked cautiously back in the direction of the house, and slid down an embankment until he was near the water. He made his way up along the creek, concealing himself behind the willows along the edge.

He worked his way carefully toward the house until he was within fifty or sixty feet of the horses. The house was another thirty feet beyond. He crouched here under the willows, peering out through the leaves, but he could see nothing.

Evidently, Bagley had gone into the house, too, to meet with the others. Mulvane knew three of the people in the house, but the fourth he did not know as yet. He stared at the chestnut horse, watching until the animal's flank was revealed, and then he read the brand on the hip. It was the brand of a local livery stable in town, a big "W" with a bar at the top and bottom. The man who had ridden this horse out here had rented the animal for the day.

Mulvane crouched where he was for about fifteen minutes wondering if he ought to creep up to the house, but he didn't like the idea of eavesdropping on Hannah Carrington. A vague suspicion was beginning to awaken inside of him, however.

Hannah had intimated that she looked upon Ward Bryant with the greatest contempt, yet she was having a secret meeting with him out here with Sheriff Bagley, and with a fourth party.

When the four of them finally came out of the house, Mulvane was not too much surprised to learn that the fourth man was Arno Quill. He couldn't hear what they were saying from the distance, but they talked for some moments near the horses, and then Bagley and Quill mounted and headed south and east toward Rawdon, while Ward Bryant and Hannah rode west in the direction of Box C.

When they were gone, Mulvane rolled over on his back and lay where he was, his arms folded beneath his head, staring up through the leafy roof of the willows.

It did not take him too long to fit some of the parts of this puzzle together. Hannah had informed on Ward Bryant and Arno Quill, but at the same time she had been working with them, along with Bagley. These four had concocted some kind of plan, the details of which Mulvane could guess, but there was no doubt in his mind that the four of them were planning some kind of deal which would circumvent the plans of the Cattleman's Association.

Hannah's trying to turn his gun against Ward Bryant meant only one thing, however. She was not only double-crossing the Cattleman's Association by working with Quill, but she was also double-crossing Quill and Bryant at the same time!

She'd lied to him about the two men, but she knew they were meeting together because she'd been at the meetings, making plans with them. Now she was making plans for herself. She'd asked for his assistance, but only for her own ends. What she had in mind he did not know as yet, but that she was a scheming, conniving woman, with a tremendous amount of ambition, he now knew.

Lying on his back under the willows he tried to figure his next move. He considered tipping off Harder and the other cattlemen as to exactly what was going on, and then riding away from here, forgetting the entire business. He wondered suddenly if Harder, himself, were double-crossing somebody else!

There seemed to be very few honest men in and about Rawdon, with the possible exception of the hired killers, Mulvane and Rudabaugh!

After awhile he got up, and he walked back to where he'd tied the claybank, and stepped into the saddle. Riding slowly back toward Rawdon he tried not to dwell upon the fact that Hannah Carrington, who had dined with him and smiled at him, probably had had a hand in the move which had brought Rudabaugh to this town.

Riding back to Rawdon, Mulvane was still not quite sure as to his next step. When he entered town and went to the hotel, he found the clerk had an envelope waiting for him with his name on it.

Taking it upstairs to his room, Mulvane opened the envelope and found the five-hundred-dollar check he'd returned to John Harder. Harder had dropped it off again at the hotel, implying that Mulvane had already earned this portion of the money they'd promised to him. He knew, then, that he owed it to Harder and to the others to tell them what was going on in case something did happen to him. He was employed by the Cattleman's Association to hold off the nesters, and because he'd taken their money, he had an obligation to work with them—and it was an obligation which could not wait.

He had a quick, light supper at the hotel, eating quite early in the evening before Ruby Watkins came out to wait on the tables. When he'd finished he went back to the stable and saddled the claybank again.

As he led the animal out of the alley, the little hostler said to him, "Reckon you're movin' around a lot these days, Mr. Mulvane."

"You move," Mulvane told him, "and you stay alive. Stand still, and you're dead."

"Makes sense," the hostler chuckled.

It was about a half-hour ride out to John Harder's Circle H, and when Mulvane arrived, the little gray-haired rancher had just finished his supper, and was sitting on the porch smoking a pipe.

Down by the bunkhouse, Mulvane spotted several of the Circle H riders lounging near the door, smoking and chatting in low tones.

Harder said when Mulvane rode up and dismounted, "Who is this?"

Mulvane stepped into the light from the open doorway.

"Come and set," Harder invited. "You pick up that check at the hotel?"

"Got it," Mulvane nodded.

"Then there's something else on your mind," Harder observed.

Mulvane said to him, "You ever hear Ward Bryant make any statement that he wanted to leave this territory?"

Harder took the pipe from his mouth, and looked at him. Mulvane had sat down on the top step of the porch, and was looking down toward the bunkhouse.

"Bryant leave?" Harder asked. "Reckon he's

doing pretty well out there at Rocking Chair. He sells out, he's as crazy as hell."

"What about Miss Carrington?" Mulvane asked him.

"Same deal," Harder told him. "Both are making money; both have good rangeland, and they'd be crazy to sell out to anyone."

"To the nesters?" Mulvane asked him, "if they got their price?"

Harder came up out of the rocking chair in which he was sitting, leaving it rock behind him. He put his shoulder against one of the porch pillars and looked down at Mulvane on the step, and then he said slowly, "You're trying to tell me something, Mulvane. Let's have it all the way now."

Mulvane told him about Hannah Carrington's asking him to watch Ward Bryant, and then of the meeting he'd planned between Bryant and Quill at the Whiting place.

Harder said slowly when Mulvane told him that, "Reckon if Quill came out after he received that note, he was coming to meet Bryant. That kind of puts Bryant in with Quill the way I look at it."

"More to it," Mulvane told him, and he went on to tell of his seeing the four at the Whiting place this afternoon. When he'd finished he said, "Bagley's in with Quill and Bryant. How would you figure Hannah's in on this deal?"

John Harder didn't speak for some time, and Mulvane knew that he'd been shocked by the revelation. Harder said finally, "I'm a bachelor, Mulvane. I don't know how a woman's mind works. Reckon Hannah's got something in mind, though."

"You figure they're both selling out to the nesters?"

Harder shook his head emphatically. "Hannah wouldn't pull out of this country," he stated quietly. "She's got cattle in her blood, and Bryant would be a damned fool to sell out at this time. There's plenty to be made in cattle if we're able to keep these farmers off the range." He paused, and then said, "Bagley's in with them, too. I might have known that. Bagley's taking our money, and anybody else's money he can get his hands on. He'd double-cross his own mother if he could make a dollar."

Mulvane said softly, "What about Hannah Carrington?"

"Hard to believe that," the rancher told him. "How does it look to you?"

"I figure she was in on it with Bryant and Quill in the beginning," Mulvane told him, "but now she has ideas of her own, and she's going it alone. She said she thought Bryant was selling out the nesters. You don't think he is."

"Can't see it that way," Harder scowled. "Can't see either one of them selling."

146

"Still they're meeting with Arno Quill," Mulvane smiled as he got up and leaned against the other post. "Reckon that means they're making up some kind of deal, doesn't it?"

"They wouldn't be meeting with that side-winder for social reasons," Harder grated, "and secretly, too. I've noticed that neither Bryant nor Hannah Carrington speaks to the man in public. As far as I know they don't know him any more than I do." He looked at Mulvane quietly, and then he said, "You're sure that you saw the four of them together?"

"I was close enough," Mulvane assured him. "There was no mistake." He leaned against the porch pillar, staring down at the wooden floor for a moment, and then he said slowly, "What do you figure would happen if Bryant and Quill, had their hired gun hand down me, then let Quill move his nesters all over this range?"

Harder thought for a moment. "The smaller ranchers would be squeezed out pretty quick," he said, "and the others would have rough going when they started to put up their fences and cut up the range."

Mulvane said, "Supposing Quill and Bryant had made a deal to let the nesters take over the range with the understanding that they would not move in on Rocking Chair or Box C. Then supposing Bryant and Hannah Carrington were to begin buying up all the ranchers who were being forced out. What would happen in the long run?"

John Harder said slowly, "Reckon they'd be big enough and strong enough, then, to run the nesters out of the country, and take the whole business, lock, stock and barrel."

Mulvane nodded. "That's how I'm beginning to look at it. Bryant could have cooked it up with this Quill to bring the emigrants here just for this reason, and Hannah Carrington was in with them at the start of it. Now it could be that she's trying to squeeze even Bryant out and take it all for herself."

Harder had one thing to say when Mulvane finished. "They've cut off a big chaw," he growled, "and I don't figure they can swallow it."

"Figured you ought to know," Mulvane told him, "in case somebody like Rudabaugh were to knock me down." He added, "There's not much you can go on, though. You don't have any proof of anything."

"Reckon we might get some proof out of this man, Quill," Harder said slowly. "We might be able to make him crack."

"I figured Quill was the man, too," Mulvane nodded. "We could bring him out here and make him talk with a little coaxing."

"Like a hot branding iron stuck under his nose," Harder grated. "He'd squeal like a pig if I know the man right. We might have a hard time getting him out here, though."

"He'd come out," Mulvane smiled, "with a gun in his back. I could bring him out here tomorrow night with no one the wiser."

"I could send some of my boys," Harder said, "but I reckon you can handle it better than they could."

Mulvane tugged at the brim of his hat. "Have him here tomorrow night," he promised, and he walked down to the tie rack, unloosened the claybank, and stepped into the saddle.

He rode back toward Rawdon under the stars, taking his time because the night was still young. He was remembering as he rode along that this was Friday night, the night of the dance in town, and Ruby Watkins had wanted him to go. He wondered if she'd gone with someone else. He wished she had, and then he wished she hadn't. It was very foolish.

He rode on through the night, the starlight revealing the trace ahead of him, and he was nearly halfway back to town when he heard the rider coming up behind him. He listened carefully even though he knew that it was probably a rider from one of the ranches coming in for the dance tonight. He'd learned through the years, however, to take every necessary precaution, to constantly anticipate the worst.

He could hear the rider coming closer at a leisurely pace, and he was about to dismiss the matter when he definitely heard another rider moving up slowly on his left, a short distance back from the trace, concealed from sight by a long, low ridge. He knew, then, that the man behind him was not going to a dance, unless it was the dance of death!

Chapter 11

There was no moon tonight, but the starlight was much too bright for him. Riding along the trace he was high up, outlined against the sky, and a good target for a gun.

As he listened he heard a third rider coming along on the right side of him, and he knew beyond any shadow of doubt that he was being trailed, and that in a matter of moments the three men behind him would close in for the kill.

Already, the two men on either side had gone on ahead of him, and they would now begin to close in, cutting him off from the town. He was quite sure that he'd been trailed from Rawdon to the Harder ranch, and now they were going to chop him down if they could.

Mulvane drew his gun in readiness, and then he touched his spurs to the claybank, and the surprised animal shot ahead very suddenly, snorting as Mulvane whipped him forward.

He ran the claybank at top speed through the night for about fifty yards, hearing his three pursuers coming on after him, making no attempt now to conceal the fact that they were trailing him. In a matter of moments he saw one of the riders break out over a ridge, and cut down toward the trace.

He had his choice now. He could drive straight toward Rawdon, breaking past the two men who were coming in on him from the sides—this they evidently anticipated. His sudden burst of speed had enabled him to elude his pursuers if he so desired. In doing so, though, he would have them at his rear, and he would be risking a bullet in the back. He didn't like the idea of running, either. The alternative, then, was to turn and fight. When he made this decision he acted swiftly and without hesitation.

Behind him a rider was coming on at breakneck speed. Mulvane suddenly pulled up the claybank, jerked the animal around, and headed him back up the trace directly at the oncoming rider.

He crouched low in the saddle now, gun in hand, as the two horses drew near to each other. The sudden maneuver had caught the rear man by surprise, and Mulvane was on top of him almost before he was aware that he was no longer the attacker, but the attacked!

Mulvane whirled the claybank away when they were on top of each other, and he fired twice, seeing the man on the other horse lifting his gun hurriedly. The rider plunged from the saddle, and Mulvane kept going up the trace.

He rode for another half mile, and then he pulled up in a grove of trees off the trace.

Dismounting, he waited here, letting the clay-bank breathe. He listened carefully for some time, hearing nothing, and he was sure that the other two men had stopped to pick up the third man who'd been shot, and they had gone back to where they'd come from.

Mulvane could only guess where they'd come from, and his guess was that they were Rocking Chair riders who'd been promised a big bonus if they could knock him down.

He waited fully forty-five minutes in the grove before stepping into the saddle and going on again toward Rawdon. If they were still lying in wait for him they would not expect him to take the trace into town, so he rode down the trace.

He saw neither horse nor rider, and in a matter of minutes he picked up the lights of Rawdon, and came down the grade into town. He wondered grimly how many more men Bryant would send after him before coming himself.

Bryant was not afraid of him, but Bryant had a great deal at stake now, and he considered it foolishness to try match guns with a loose gun hand, whose life or death meant nothing to anyone.

It was past ten o'clock in the evening when he returned to Rawdon. As he stepped into the hotel, he saw Ruby Watkins sitting in a corner of the lounge, pretending to be reading a paper.

When she saw him she put the paper down,

and Mulvane went over to sit beside her. He said slowly, "You didn't go to the dance?"

"No," she said.

"Why not?" he asked.

She shrugged. "No one asked me to go," she said, but he knew that this was not exactly the truth, because on a night like this at least half a dozen young riders would have been in here, asking her to go with them. They'd seen her in town, and they knew about her.

"Where were you?" Ruby asked him.

"Had to ride out to see one of the ranchers," Mulvane explained.

"More trouble?" she asked.

Mulvane shrugged. "Always trouble in this business," he said. "It ends when you're dead."

He wondered as he sat in the lobby about the man who'd tried to kill him on the trace. He knew he'd hit the man, but he didn't think his bullets had killed.

Ruby was saying, "Why won't you go to the dance with me tonight?"

Mulvane smiled. "No place for a man like me," he said. "That crowd wouldn't feel right with me around, anyway."

"If you won't take me to the dance tonight," Ruby said, "maybe you'd care to take me riding tomorrow. Mr. Wolsey has given me the afternoon off."

Mulvane smiled. "Reckon we can arrange that,"

he said. "I'll pick you up right after dinner."

The warmth came into her eyes, then, and she said, "I'll be ready, Mr. Mulvane."

She went to her room off the kitchen, and Mulvane went upstairs. Before he entered his room this time, however, he kicked in the door, stepping to one side as he did so. Having satisfied himself that the room was empty, he walked in, pulled down the blind, and then lighted the lamp, making sure that he was not silhouetted against the window.

As he took off his boots he was wondering why he had made the date with Ruby Watkins. In a very short while now, this whole affair would be wound up one way or another, and he would either be dead or on his way to some other place. A man on the loose such as himself could not tie himself down to a woman—any woman. It was not fair to the woman.

When he slept that night he slept with his gun within reach, and he slept with a chair jammed against the door knob so that it could not be broken in without him hearing it.

He idled his way through the next morning, and then at noon he rented a buckboard from a livery stable at the other end of town and drove it down to the hotel. He knew that people were watching him as he went into the hotel to wait for Ruby.

When she came into the dining room, Mulvane stared at her in amazement. She was dressed in a beautiful, highly-expensive green brocade dress, trimmed with gold, and she wore a very lovely Princess Eugenie hat with a green feather in it.

In this costume she looked like an altogether different girl. She was grown up, strikingly beautiful, and for a moment, looking at her, Mulvane could not speak.

Ruby was grinning at him, and then she explained the change.

"Mr. Wolsey has a whole trunkful of clothes like these up in the attic," she said. "It seems one of his guests left town without paying her bill, and he was left with her clothes. He told me to help myself. Mr. Wolsey is very kind."

"You're grown up," Mulvane told her. "Suddenly, you're grown up!"

Ruby put her hand on his arm, and they walked out to the porch like that, and then Mulvane helped her up to the seat of the buckboard. He took the reins, and they drove east out of town.

As he drove through the street he saw Arno Quill standing in front of the barber shop, and he remembered that tonight he had a little business with Quill, and that business would quite probably bring this whole affair to a head.

Ruby was saying, "When was the last time you took a girl riding, Mr. Mulvane?"

"When I was young," Mulvane smiled. "I don't know how many years ago. It was a long way back."

"You must have been a handsome boy," Ruby smiled. "I wish I could have known you, then." She added quickly, "I'm glad, though, that I know you now, too."

"How are you getting on at the hotel?" Mulvane asked her, changing the subject.

"I like it," Ruby nodded, "but I won't stay there forever, waiting on tables."

"What would you do?" Mulvane asked curiously.

"I might open a dress shop when I have enough money," Ruby said, "or a hat shop, or maybe a store for children's clothes. I would buy all the clothes back east and bring them back here to sell at a profit."

"If your nester friends take over the country," Mulvane smiled at her, "you wouldn't make a nickel. In cattle country you might make out because the cattlemen are making money."

"It wouldn't have to be this town," Ruby admitted. "It might be any town, anywhere."

"I think you'd make out," Mulvane nodded. "You have a good head."

"Thank you," Ruby smiled.

They gave the grove in which the nester wagons were located a wide berth, and then they rode up along the creek, following a trace which led out to one of the ranches.

"If your friends saw you now," Mulvane told her, nodding toward the grove, "they wouldn't know you in a million years."

157

"They'll never see me again," Ruby said slowly. "My uncle would work me to death the way he's worked his wife. I'll never go back."

"You won't," Mulvane promised.

"Then you'll have to marry me," Ruby smiled. "I don't see any other way out." She put her hand on his arm as they rode along in silence.

Once a rider came in their direction, moving down the trace, and as he did so, Mulvane kept his hand on his gun, watching the man all the while until he'd ridden past. He was thinking as the rider moved out of sight that this was the way it would be all the time. It was not a good way to be, and to be a husband.

They drove back late in the afternoon, and Ruby was reluctant to get back to the hotel and put on her waitress dress and go back to serving tables.

Mulvane said to her, "Some day you'll own dresses like that."

"I hope so," Ruby smiled. "Thanks for taking me out, Mr. Mulvane."

"My pleasure," Mulvane nodded.

When he had his supper that night, Ruby waited on him as usual, and she was in good spirits as she moved around the dining room.

As Mulvane finished his meal he wondered if Arno Quill would come in for supper. Sitting at the table, too, he made his plans for getting Quill out to Harder's ranch.

After he paid his bill Mulvane went around

back to the stable where he found the little hostler sitting on a bale of hay, smoking a pipe, and he made his deal with the man.

He wanted the claybank saddled and waiting for him down at the west end of town beyond the farthest house, and he wanted a spare horse with the claybank.

"I don't want anybody seeing you going down there," he told the old man as he slipped him a few dollars. "Don't take the horses down the street."

"How soon you want 'em there?" the hostler asked.

"Take them down now," Mulvane told him.

"Want me to wait with them?" the old man asked.

Mulvane shook his head. "Somebody might ask questions if they find you with my horse. I don't want any questions asked or answered."

The old man nodded again. "You're the boss, Mr. Mulvane," he said.

Mulvane left the stable then, and walked back to the porch, wondering if Quill were still in his room. When he came up on the porch, however, and glanced through the window to the dining room, he saw Quill just sitting down at one of the tables. He knew, then, what he would do, and he knew, also, that it was going to much easier than he'd anticipated.

Moving back to the stables again he found the old man saddling the claybank, and he said,

"Hurry it up." He waited until the hostler had saddled the two horses and was leading them away, across a vacant lot beyond, then he stepped up to the kitchen door and opened it.

The cook, a fat man with a dirty apron, looked at him in surprise, and Mulvane said easily, "Waiting to see Miss Watkins."

He closed the door and leaned against it, waiting for Ruby to come back to the kitchen with her order. There had been several people in the dining room, and Ruby was now probably taking their orders.

She came into the kitchen, moving briskly, and when she saw him she stopped in surprise. Mulvane motioned for her to come over, and when she stepped to his side she said quickly, "Anything wrong, Mr. Mulvane?"

"I want you to do something for me," he told her. "Quill is dining in there. Tell him Sheriff Bagley wants to see him at the rear door of the kitchen right away. Tell him to come through the kitchen if he wants to."

Ruby's eyes widened. "Are you going to shoot him?" she asked.

Mulvane smiled. "Not as bad as that," he said. "Tell him Bagley said it was important, and to hurry."

Ruby nodded, and headed back toward the dining room. Mulvane stepped outside into the darkness, drawing his gun when he was back in

160

the shadows. He didn't think Quill would have any particular suspicions of anything happening to him in town, and he might be curious as to why Bagley wanted to see him.

Mulvane saw the old man coming back from his short trip to the edge of town with the two horses, and he knew that everything was now in readiness. Then the door opened, and Quill stood in the doorway, framed there for a moment very foolishly. A man with any brains, and with any knowledge of this country, and involved the way Quill was, should never have stood in an open doorway where he could have been shot down without warning.

Quill said softly, "Bagley?"

Then he stepped out into the night, closing the door behind him. As he did so, Mulvane stepped up beside him, jamming the muzzle of the gun into the small man's back, and saying gently, "You know me, Quill."

"I'm not armed," Quill mumbled. "You know I don't carry a gun, Mulvane."

"Just keep walking," Mulvane told him, "and you won't have any trouble."

He moved Quill past the stable and then back around the stable, following the path the hostler had taken a few minutes before. They walked in the darkness beyond the lights of the houses along the street, Mulvane still holding his gun against Quill's back as he prodded the man forward.

"A hell of a business," Quill growled once. "You got no call to do this, Mulvane."

"Open your mouth," Mulvane told him, "and you'll be dead back here in the vacant lots, and nobody giving a damn."

Quill said no more until they came up to where the two horses were tied, and then he said in surprise, "We're going away?"

"We're taking a ride," Mulvane said. "Somebody wants to see you. Get on the horse."

"Who?"

"Get on the horse," Mulvane snapped at him, and Quill climbed into the saddle, glancing back toward the town as he did so. Then Mulvane slapped the flank of the horse, and they rode off with Quill a little ahead of him.

"Where are we going?" Quill asked.

"You'll find out pretty soon," Mulvane told him. He turned Quill's horse off the road, and up into the hills where there was little possibility that they would meet anyone.

They rode on, Quill silent now, and evidently very much puzzled. He asked no questions until they raised the lights of Harder's Circle H a half-hour later, and then he said suspiciously, "Who's ranch is that?"

"You'll find out," Mulvane smiled.

They rode down the slope and up to the ranch-house, finding John Harder waiting for them on the porch.

"Any trouble?" Harder asked as Mulvane dismounted.

"He's here," Mulvane said.

Quill was still up on his horse, and he looked down and said, "Who's that?"

"Get off the horse," Harder snapped.

Mulvane tied the claybank to the tie rack, and then he sat down on the porch.

Quill got down off his horse, blustering. "There's law and order in this town," he growled. "You boys can't push me around like this."

Harder said to him, "Sit down, you tinhorn."

Quill went up on the porch and sat down in a wicker chair there. Harder was in a rocker, rocking gently as he spoke. He said without emotion, "What's the deal between you and Bryant and Miss Carrington?"

Mulvane saw Quill's head jerk around as he stared at the rancher. "Mr. Ward Bryant, owner of Rocking Chair?"

"You know damned well who I mean," Harder snapped. "What's the deal between you two?"

"There's no deal," Quill said quickly. "I don't even know the man."

"How about Miss Carrington?"

"I've seen her in town," Quill shrugged. "That's all I know, mister."

"And Bagley?" Harder said slowly.

"That one's your man," Quill grinned. "You boys know that."

"You haven't made a deal with any of them?" Harder said.

"What kind of deal?" Quill countered.

"A deal to bring in your damned nesters," Harder grated, "and drive the ranchers out of this country, and then let Bryant and Miss Carrington gobble everything up. That's the deal I'm talking about, mister. How much did they pay you to come out here with that crowd in the grove?"

"You're crazy," Quill spluttered. "You're crazy as hell."

"That's all you have to say?" Harder asked him.

"What else can I say?" Quill mumbled.

"Maybe you'll say something else later," Harder smiled grimly. "On your feet, mister."

"Where are we going?" Quill asked him.

"Down by the corral," Harder snapped. "Move on."

Mulvane got up and followed the two of them as they walked down toward the shadowy corral which was about twenty-five yards from the porch. There were three men waiting there.

Harder said as he came up, "Kick that fire up, boys."

One of the riders stepped over to the fire and poked at it with a piece of wood, and then tossed some more chunks of wood in among the embers, making it blaze up again.

"Got an iron ready?" Harder asked.

"Ready," one of the riders said laconically.

"Snub this critter up to that corral post," Harder ordered, nodding his head toward Quill who was staring at the fire, fascinated.

"What are you going to do?" Quill asked slowly.

Two of the Circle H men grabbed Quill by the arms, jerking him back toward the post. They had a rope ready, and they quickly bound him to the post so that he could not move.

Another man had put one of the branding irons into the fire, and was standing there looking at it thoughtfully. Harder said to his men, "That's it, boys," and the three men moved back toward the bunkhouse. "You hear any yelling down here," he called after them, "don't pay any attention. It'll be just a pig squealing."

The firelight flickered upon Quill tied to the post, and Mulvane could see the terrible fear coming into the small man's eyes, and he mumbled, "You're not going to put that brand on me, mister."

Harder said, "You sure you don't know anything about a deal with Ward Bryant?"

Quill hesitated this time. "You're crazy," he growled. "How the hell would I know anything about Ward Bryant?"

"I'm asking you," Harder said. "Reckon you're the one knows, mister."

"I don't know anything," Quill scowled, but he was staring at the fire as Mulvane went over

165

to it to push the branding iron deeper down into the hot coals. Then Mulvane walked over to the corral fence to sit on the top of the rail. He rolled a cigarette there in the light of the fire, and he put it in his mouth.

Harder was now squatting near the fire, watching the iron, and he had nothing more to say. Quill looked at Harder, and then at Mulvane up on the rail, and he said slowly, "Reckon you boys better cut me loose."

Neither Harder nor Mulvane said anything.

"How the hell would I know Ward Bryant?" Quill asked. "You're both crazy." There was a note of hysteria in his voice now.

Mulvane touched a match to his cigarette, and then he said to Harder, "Reckon she's hot enough now, Mr. Harder."

John Harder pulled the branding iron from the fire, and Mulvane could see the round, red-hot circle with the H in the middle of it. Mulvane said, "Where you going to burn him?"

"Chest, first," Harder said without any emotion. "Reckon we'll start there, Mulvane, and work around a little."

Cigarette in mouth, Mulvane slid down from the corral rail and walked over to the trembling Quill. Grasping the man's shirt front with both hands, he yanked hard, ripping it open, baring him almost to the waist, and revealing his flabby, white skin.

"Come and get him," he said to Harder, and the

rancher took the branding iron from the fire, and turned and walked toward Quill.

Quill was breathing heavily now, the sweat pouring down his face. He looked at Mulvane, and he said, "You're not going to let him do this to me, are you, mister?"

Mulvane shrugged. "Reckon I work for the Cattleman's Association," he said. "Harder is head of it."

Harder said, "Enough damned talk."

He held the branding iron up, and he moved closer to Quill, aiming it at Quill's quivering chest. Quill strained at the ropes, the sweat dripping from his chin now, his face reddish in the light of the hot iron. His eyes were wild. He said, "Listen—listen—!"

"What's the deal with Bryant?" Harder asked him. "This is the last time, mister."

The branding iron was less than six inches from Quill's chest, and the fat man tried to bore back into the post.

"What's the deal, Quill?" Harder repeated.

Quill was sagging on the ropes now, his face livid, and his mouth open. "All right," he mumbled. "All right. I'm not getting burned for anybody."

"We're listening," Harder said. "Get it over with, man."

"He hired me," Quill gasped. "He and Miss Carrington. Bagley's in it, too."

"Where'd you meet him?" Harder asked.

"Kansas City," Quill said. He was still staring at the hot iron in Harder's hands as if unable to take his eyes off it. "I met him in Kansas City. We made the deal."

"You were to round up this bunch of farmers," Mulvane said to him, "and bring them out here."

Quill nodded. "I've lined up emigrant outfits before," he was saying. "Bryant knew about this. He was paying me a thousand dollars to bring them out. I was to pass the word among the nesters, though, that they weren't to settle on Rocking Chair or Box C range."

Mulvane said, "You sure Miss Carrington was in it?"

"Damn sure," Quill snarled. "She's as bad as Bryant. Wouldn't be surprised if the whole deal was hers to begin with. They want to run this whole county, mister. They're going to drive all you ranchers out, and then when you're gone they'll turn on the nesters one by one, and make it too hot for them to stay here."

"What about Rudabaugh?" Mulvane asked.

"Bryant or Bagley brought him in," Quill muttered. "I didn't have anything to do with that, mister."

"What about the men who tried to kill me?" Mulvane snapped.

"My job," Quill told him, "was to bring these damned farmers here, and get them scattered out over this range in the right places. That's all I know about it. When the Cattleman's Association brought you in, I guess Bryant figured he had to get rid of you some way, and he couldn't do it, himself, because he's a rancher, too."

"That's all you know?" Harder said.

He walked back to the fire and dropped the iron on the ground.

"That's all I know," Quill mumbled.

"That's all you'll ever know, too," Mulvane smiled. "You won't last twenty-four hours in Rawdon when Bryant learns you've talked."

Harder came back and said, "Cut him loose, Mulvane."

Mulvane took a knife from his pocket and cut the ropes. Quill staggered away a few steps, and then sat down on the ground, his back against one of the corral posts.

"They'll kill me," he muttered.

Mulvane said, "You're through in this country, mister. Don't ever come back to it." He said to Harder, "I don't want him going back to Rawdon, either. He might tip somebody off as to what happened here tonight."

Harder nodded. "I'll have one of my boys ride with him up to Flat Rock station, fifty miles from here. We'll see him on the train back east."

He went up, then, to talk to one of his riders at the bunkhouse. In a short while two horses were saddled, and Quill was on his way.

Mulvane sat on the porch with Harder, both men staring out into the darkness, silent for the moment, and then Harder said slowly, "Any way you look at it, it's a damnable trick."

"Now you know what you're up against," Mulvane told him. "What's your next move?"

"Have to call a secret meeting of the ranchers without Bryant and Miss Carrington," Harder said. "Reckon the other boys have a right to know what the hell's been going on."

"What about the nesters?" Mulvane asked him.

"They'll have to be told, too," Harder stated. "Some of them might have enough sense in their heads to believe it, and move on to some place where they're more welcome."

"I'll take care of the nesters," Mulvane said. "Maybe they won't believe me, but I'll tell them."

Harder said, "I'll send one of my boys out now. We'll have a meeting out here early in the morning, and then we'll put it up to Bryant."

"What do you think he'll do?" Mulvane asked curiously.

"He can't fight all of us," Harder scowled. "We'll tell him this country's not healthy for him any more. We don't want him or his stock in the roundups, and that he'd better move out. The same goes for Miss Hannah Carrington."

"Might take more than talk," Mulvane observed. "Bryant looks like a tough one to me."

"He's tough," Harder admitted, "but he can't buck all of us, and that's what he'll have to do if he stays in this country."

Mulvane said as he got up, "I'll talk to the nesters in the morning. Maybe when they find out Quill is gone, they won't have enough heart to keep up the fight. They might move, then, whether they believe me or not."

"My advice to you," Harder said quietly, "is to stay away from Ward Bryant until the ranchers have decided what they're going to do. Bryant will hold you personally responsible for ruining his plans. He'll never let you leave the country alive."

"I'll watch him," Mulvane nodded.

He rode back to Rawdon, watching his back trail as he rode. He was thinking of Hannah Carrington, wondering how it was possible that a girl with her beauty and intelligence could be so consumed by avarice and greed as to betray the friends and neighbors who'd probably known her all her life.

She'd tried to use him, too, and he remembered that in the beginning he'd been taken in by her. He was grateful now that she hadn't gotten too much of a hold on him. She was a doomed woman.

Chapter 12

Back in town Mulvane stopped in at the Great Western Saloon, seeing some of the nesters there, bitter-faced, glum, and almost without hope now. He was quite sure when he explained to them what had happened, and how they'd been duped by Arno Quill, they would pack up their wagons and roll out of the grove. Possibly, somewhere they would find land—good land—where they could raise their crops in peace and happiness.

As Mulvane was at the bar, Bagley came in, hauling up alongside of him. Mulvane looked at the lawman, unsmilingly, and then he said, "How's Rudabaugh?"

Bagley shrugged. "Reckon he should be up and around in a day or two." He added, "I've checked that fellow with Washington, and I found that he really is a fake."

Mulvane lifted his glass. "Plenty of fakes in this town," he said.

Bagley just rubbed his round chin, and Mulvane was glad when the lawman finished his drink and moved off.

Stepping out into the street, Mulvane turned

left and walked directly down to the house Rudabaugh had been taken to the day before. He knocked and a woman opened the door.

"Friend to see Mr. Rudabaugh," he said.

The woman frowned at him, but let him in, and he went up a narrow staircase to the second floor.

"First door at the left off the landing," the woman said.

Mulvane paused at the door, and then knocked gently. He heard Rudabaugh's voice tell him to come in. He was quite sure Rudabaugh had had no visitors with the exception of Quill. Rudabaugh probably thought Quill was at the door now.

When Mulvane stepped into the room Rudabaugh was sitting in a chair near the window, with the blind drawn down, and he was in the process of cleaning his gun. There was a bandage around his head, and his thin face was more pale than ever—the face of a ghost.

When he saw Mulvane he started to get up from the chair, and he looked toward a closet where Mulvane assumed he had another gun in a suitcase.

Mulvane said to him, "I'm not gunning for you, Rudabaugh."

The lean man sat down slowly, watching Mulvane. He rubbed the muzzle of his gun with an oily rag, and then he pushed a piece of the rag inside the barrel and worked it up and down with a steel rod.

"What brings you here?" he asked gruffly.

"Friendly visit," Mulvane told him. "Want me to send down for a couple of drinks?"

Rudabaugh just looked at him, and then he picked up a small bell on the dresser nearby, and he shook it. In a moment the woman who had let Mulvane into the house opened the door, and Rudabaugh said:

"Tell that old man who runs the errands for me to pick up a bottle of whiskey and two glasses."

The woman went out without a word, and Mulvane sat down on the edge of the bed. "How's your head?" he asked.

"I'm alive," Rudabaugh told him, "and I expect to be out of this room tomorrow."

Mulvane shrugged. "There's no rush," he said. "You won't be going anywhere."

"I'll be looking for you," Rudabaugh told him. "Reckon you know that." Mulvane nodded.

"You were lucky the last time," Rudabaugh said reflectively. "My slug was half an inch too high, and yours was a little lower. That's how lucky you were."

Mulvane smiled. "The lucky man wins with a gun the way he wins at cards," he said. "When the luck's your way, no one can beat you. When it's the other way, you're gone."

"This time," Rudabaugh told him, "it'll run my way."

Mulvane watched him working on the gun, and then he propped a pillow against the back of his head and leaned back, lifting his boots to the top of the bedstead. He said, "How much they pay you for this job, Rudabaugh?"

"None of your damned business," Rudabaugh snapped. "You're not getting anything out of me, Mulvane."

"Figured you'd like to know," Mulvane said. "Your man, Quill, ran out on you."

Rudabaugh looked at him now, and he stopped working on the gun.

"He's gone," Mulvane said. "Figured the odds were getting a little tough, and he's out of it. Where does that leave you?"

"I'll look you up now for sure," Rudabaugh said, "whether there's money in it or not. You know that."

Mulvane smiled. "I'm not anxious to kill you," he stated. "That's why I'm here tonight."

"I have to kill *you*," Rudabaugh said. He went back to cleaning the gun, and after awhile he said, "What makes you think Quill ran out?"

"Ask for him at the hotel tomorrow," Mulvane said. "He's gone."

He wondered how much this man knew about the deal between Quill and Bryant. There was the good possibility Rudabaugh didn't even know about Bryant, and that he'd been hired by Quill directly. Quill could have lied about that part of it.

"You'd be smarter," Mulvane said, "to ride out of here. There's no money in it for you now. Only a damned fool would stay around."

Rudabaugh touched the bandage around his head. "This keeps me here, Mulvane."

Mulvane murmured, "I almost wish you were doing it for the money, Rudabaugh."

"You talk like a damned fool," Rudabaugh said quietly, and then the old man came in with the bottle and the glasses, and they had their drink.

After awhile Mulvane left, leaving the killer cleaning his gun, preparing for the encounter which now was inevitable. He went back to the hotel with the knowledge that tomorrow Rudabaugh would be on the street, and tomorrow, also, he was going to inform the nesters what had happened, and tomorrow Ward Bryant would know him, and would be looking for him.

He slept soundly in his hotel room that night, knowing that on the morrow he would need all of his faculties, all the craft and all the skill he'd acquired over the years.

He slept late, too, because there was no particular reason for rising early. When he got up, he shaved leisurely, calling for hot water from below, and then he went downstairs for his breakfast.

The morning had been dark and foreboding, with the hint of rain in the air. By the time he'd shaved and come downstairs, the rain had started to fall. Mulvane was remembering that it was on just this kind of day that he'd arrived in Rawdon, and the chances were that he'd be leaving the same way—if he left at all.

He had no doubt that Rudabaugh would be looking for him within a matter of minutes or hours. Bryant would be learning of Quill's defection and confession sometime this day, also, and Mulvane hoped that he would be able to have it out with Rudabaugh before Bryant came into town.

Ruby said as he came into the dining room, "You're late this morning, Mr. Mulvane."

Mulvane nodded, and he wondered about her, too, after this day. "No rush today," he said.

He stepped to one of the dining room windows, and he looked out at the rain. As he watched he saw a boy come out of the telegraph office, and run down along the boardwalk until he came to Sheriff Bagley's office. Then he ducked inside with his message. He'd been carrying a yellow telegram slip in his hand.

Mulvane stood there, watching, wondering if Bagley had really sent a wire to Washington to check on Rudabaugh. It was ridiculous because Bagley was in with Bryant, and he certainly knew about Rudabaugh.

Ruby was saying, "Are you going to have breakfast, Mr. Mulvane?"

Mulvane sat down at a table near the window, and he was still wondering about the wire Bagley had received as he ordered his breakfast. It wasn't until he was having his cup of coffee, and he saw Ed Bagley riding hard out of town, that the wire began to make sense.

He knew, then, that they'd slipped up as far as Arno Quill was concerned. Quill had been put aboard a train last night, or this morning, and he could have gotten off at the next station to send a wire to Bagley, informing him that Mulvane and Harder knew of their plans. It was like Quill to do this. Quill was out of the picture now, but he still had his hatred for the men who had forced the confession out of him, and driven him from the country.

Bagley knew, now, and Bagley was riding at top speed out to Rocking Chair to inform Ward Bryant. Mulvane sipped his coffee thoughtfully, wondering what Bryant's reaction would be. Bryant would attempt to kill him, but he would know, also, that Harder and the other ranchers would be on Mulvane's side, and this might involve some difficulty.

He toyed with his breakfast this morning, sitting near the window watching the dark storm clouds sweeping in over the town. He wondered who would come first—Rudabaugh or Bryant.

Ruby Watkins paused at his table and said, "You're worried about something, Mr. Mulvane. What is it?"

"Whatever it is," Mulvane smiled at her, "there's no stopping it now."

Certain things were going to happen today which just had to happen as sure as the sun rose and set each day.

"Why don't we leave here?" Ruby said to him. "I'll go with you, Mr. Mulvane. We can get two horses and ride away, and that will be the end of it."

Mulvane stared at her. "Would you really go?" he asked softly.

"I'd go," Ruby nodded, and Mulvane was tempted for the moment. His work was finished here; he'd kept the nesters in the grove as he'd contracted to do, and he didn't think that under the circumstances they would try to move out on to the rangeland. He'd exposed Quill and Bryant and Hannah Carrington, and his job was finished.

He couldn't go with this innocent young girl, though, because he was Mulvane, and his gun was for hire, and in the line of duty he'd made many enemies in many places—men who were ready to gun him down without hesitation. He could not drag a young girl into this.

He could not conceive of himself, either, holding up in some shack out on an open range, miserably trying to make a go of it, with the

179

wanderlust always in him. It was not fair to the girl; it was not even fair to his inner self.

"Reckon I can't go, Ruby," he said gently. "I'm obliged for the offer."

"You might be dead before you go," Ruby told him miserably.

"I knew that when I came here," Mulvane smiled. "I knew the odds."

"Then go away."

Mulvane shook his head.

"You're stubborn," Ruby scowled. "You want to die."

He noticed that she was close to tears as she left the table to wait on another diner. He watched her go, knowing that he could not call her back—that he could not call any one back.

After breakfast he went into the lobby, picked up an old newspaper, and went back to his room. He sat on the edge of the bed for a while, glancing at the paper, and then he put it down and went to the window to look out.

It was now about eleven o'clock in the morning. The rain seemed to have slackened for the moment, and he was thinking that this was a good time to see the nesters.

Getting his leather jacket from the peg on the wall, he slipped it on, and then went downstairs again. It had almost stopped raining now, but there was plenty of rain left in those clouds, and he anticipated a downpour any moment.

It seemed as if the rain, too, were waiting for something, and when Mulvane stepped out into the street he had the feeling that this whole town was waiting for something to happen.

A chill, damp wind blew down from the ranges to the west as Mulvane moved around to the stable to saddle the claybank.

The old hostler said to him as he came into the stable, "A wet one today, Mr. Mulvane."

Mulvane nodded.

"Had a day like this last spring," the old man went on reflectively. "Blew the roof off Bud Jackson's place down the street."

"That right," Mulvane murmured.

"You get this kind of look in the sky in the winter," the hostler told him, "an' you end up with six feet o' snow. Be just rain squalls today, though, I figure."

Mulvane led the claybank out of the alley, and then he stepped into the saddle, and rode slowly out toward the grove. He noticed that there were very few people out in the street this morning, and those who were out seemed to be in a hurry to get back to shelter before the rain broke again.

As he rode out to the grove he saw a buckboard moving out ahead of him, loaded down with staples which an enterprising storekeeper was taking out to the grove for possible sale.

Nearing the grove Mulvane had his moment of pity for these people who looked forward now to a chill, dreary, wet day in their damp wagons. As he rode into the grove, men were fastening down canvas sheets, and they turned to stare at him. It was the first time he'd actually entered the grove since coming to Rawdon. He saw the bitterness and hatred for him in their eyes.

He said to the nearest man, "Round up your crowd. I have something to say to them."

He saw Joab Watkins come out of one of the wagons and glare at him. The lean farmer hated him with a helpless rage.

Mulvane sat astride the claybank, waiting patiently. He knew they hated him, but they would come to listen out of curiosity, wondering what he had to say.

When the word spread through the grove that he was there, and wanted to talk, they began to come, one and two at a time, many of the women trailing after the men, and children following them.

One of the nesters growled, "What in hell you got to say to us, mister? Reckon you've done all you can do."

Mulvane looked around at them, and then he told them of Arno Quill's confession of the whole plan which Quill and Bryant had concocted to bring them out here for the purpose of getting control of the range.

They listened to him in silence until he'd finished. He said, "Quill's gone, now, and you've never had a chance, from the beginning, of settling here. You'd have broken your backs trying to get a foothold in this country, and then they would have pushed you out anyway. You'd be smart now to pull out of here, and look for another place to settle."

"It's easy to talk," one of the nesters growled.

Mulvane shrugged. He could see that some of them may have possibly believed him; others did not, and considered this just another ruse to get them on their way. Even when they learned that Quill was gone they would think he'd driven the man out.

"What about that U.S. marshal you shot up, yesterday?" Joab Watkins shouted. "You're hangin' for that, mister."

"He was a hired killer," Mulvane stated, not even looking at Watkins. "He was brought in by Bryant to kill me."

"Maybe we'll get a real marshal," another nester called bitterly. "Then you won't be able to stop us, mister."

Mulvane smiled. "You might force your way on to this range," he said, "but you'll never stay there. You'll sweat and in the end they'll drive you out."

He had no more to say to them, then, and he didn't care now whether they believed or not. At least they'd heard, and he was clear of them.

He rode back to Rawdon just as the rain started again. He didn't think he'd be using the claybank any more this day so he stabled the horse, wondering as he did so if Rudabaugh were up and about as yet.

Stepping into the hotel he was about to go to his room when he saw Hannah Carrington open her door down the hallway on the main floor. He noticed that her face was white and drawn, and she motioned for him to come over.

He realized, then, that she'd gotten the news from Bagley, meeting him on her way into town.

When Mulvane came up she said quietly, "Will you step inside, please."

Mulvane stepped into the room, and she closed the door behind him, and then as he turned around she struck him fully in the face with her hand. It was not a slap, but a punch, with the fingers tightened.

Mulvane looked down at her, a feeling of pity coming over him. She was a lost, beaten woman, and she knew it, and this was all she could do in retribution.

He said, "You've seen Bagley, and you know."

"I know," Hannah almost hissed. "I know what you've done."

"What," Mulvane asked her curiously, "were you trying to do?"

"You've pretended to be my friend," Hannah whispered, and she was almost ugly in her rage, "and all the while you've been spying upon me and working against me."

Then she punched him again, harder than the first time, drawing a little blood to his lips.

Mulvane stepped forward, then, grabbing her arms, and ramming her hard back against the wall, and pinning her there.

Looking down at her, he said quietly and softly, "You're finished, Hannah Carrington. You played the game, but you're finished."

When he stepped away from her he could see that she was through. She was beaten, and she would never be the same. There was nothing anyone could do to her to make it worse.

He left the room, and went upstairs to his own room. The rain was falling heavily now, beating a steady tattoo on the roof overhead. Stepping to the window he looked out, and he could see that the street was empty. A man was leading a buckboard hurriedly down an alley nearby, and a small boy ran out into the road to retrieve a ball which had rolled there, and then he ran back to shelter.

A half-hour later as Mulvane watched from the window he saw Ed Bagley ride in, his slicker tight around his neck, and his hat low against the rain. Bagley rode down the alley behind his office. He came out a few minutes later, but instead of going into the office, he walked hurriedly down the boardwalk to the boarding-house where Rudabaugh lived.

Mulvane had his answer, then, to one of the

questions, still unresolved in his mind. Rudabaugh had been hired by Ward Bryant, and now Bagley was calling upon the hired gun openly because it had come to that.

Strapping on his gunbelt again, Mulvane went downstairs. Looking out through the glass in the front door, he saw Ward Bryant and two men riding by. Bryant glanced at the hotel, but could not see Mulvane. Like Bagley, he was wearing a slicker, shiny with rain, and water dripped from his hat as he rode. He noticed something else about Bryant, also. The stock of a rifle stuck up from a saddle holster, protected by a canvas covering.

Bryant was in town today to hunt for bear. This was not to be one man against another, or even two or three men against another, but a man with a high-powered rifle hunting down another man and killing him in cold blood.

He watched Bryant dismount in front of Bagley's office, and then step inside. The two men with Bryant rode down the alley behind the office to stable the horses.

Mulvane watched, a thin smile on his face. The players in this little drama which was about to be enacted were moving into position, and the climax was near. Very shortly the big guns would begin to boom, and possibly for the last time for him.

Chapter 13

Mulvane stepped into the dining room, finding it empty, and he moved across to one of the windows to look out. He saw Rudabaugh and Bagley hurrying up the street toward the sheriff's office. There were to be five of them, then, and Mulvane wondered cynically where John Harder and the other ranchers were. Very possibly they were still debating what should be done about Bryant and Hannah Carrington, and while they were having their discussion Bryant would be running down the man who had exposed his plan.

Ruby Watkins came out of the kitchen, and seeing Mulvane at the window she came over and said quickly, "Is there anything wrong, Mr. Mulvane?"

Then she looked out the window, and she, too, saw Rudabaugh and Bagley approaching the sheriff's office, and she saw Bryant in the doorway, and she said, "They're here after you."

"They'll be looking for me," Mulvane told her.

"You're not going to fight them alone?" Ruby whispered.

She stared out at the rain which was driving down into the street now.

"I'll fight them," Mulvane said, "or they'll shoot me down like a dog in a back alley."

He watched Bryant talking with Bagley and Rudabaugh, and then he said, "Have to get out of here, Ruby."

He was about to step toward the kitchen with the intention of going out through the kitchen door to the rear, when he heard a voice from the lobby.

"I think you'd better stay here and face them, Mr. Mulvane."

Mulvane whirled around and stared into the blazing blue eyes of Hannah Carrington. She was in the doorway between the lobby and the dining room, holding a black derringer in her hand, the muzzle of the little gun lined on his chest.

"I think," Hannah repeated, "you'd better stay where you are. You have a lot to answer for."

Mulvane looked at her, and at the gun, and when he glanced out the window again, he could see Bryant, Rudabaugh, Bagley and the two Rocking Chair riders crossing the street, heading toward the hotel.

"Stay where you are," Hannah Carrington said.

Mulvane looked toward the kitchen door less than a dozen feet away. He knew that if he could get out there to the back of the hotel he could give them a chase for their money. He didn't relish the idea of staying here, and having them walk in and shoot him down.

He wondered if he could risk making that short distance across to the open doorway. Hannah was about thirty feet from him, and those derringers were not too accurate.

He didn't have to run, though, because Ruby Watkins, who had been listening, stepped in front of him, shielding him with her body. She said slowly, "Miss Carrington, if you shoot me they'll hang you."

She started to move carefully toward the kitchen, then, motioning for Mulvane to stay behind her. Hannah stared at the two of them, hatred blazing in her eyes, and for a moment Mulvane thought she would pull the trigger and put a bullet into the nester girl.

"You're not going to shoot," Ruby was saying calmly. "You know you're not going to shoot."

She kept edging toward the doorway, and then Mulvane stepped into the kitchen to safety. He hadn't liked the idea of hiding behind a woman, but Ruby had been right. Hannah probably could have shot him and gotten away with it on some kind of pretext, but she could not shoot another woman—a completely innocent woman like Ruby Watkins—and expect this town to let it ride.

Ward Bryant and the others had by this time reached the doorway of the hotel, and Hannah called sharply, "This way, Ward. He's in here."

Mulvane lunged for the door leading out toward the stable, and he was going out into the yard when he heard someone running across the dining room.

He raced down along the side wall of the stable, rounding it at the far end, the heavy rain drenching him as he ran. He had to stay away now, waiting for Bryant to divide his crowd. He had no chance against five guns, but if he could keep moving and stay alive, and meet up with them one or two at a time, he could possibly live through this day.

He ran up an alley which took him out to the main street, and then he cut across the street, heading for an alley between the red-brick bank building and a store. He expected no help from this town. Even if Bryant had brought in twenty men to run him down he could expect no help. They knew him for what he was—a loose gun— and they had no sympathy for him, any more than they'd had for Rudabaugh when he'd been shot down.

As Mulvane darted into the alley he heard the boom of a heavy caliber rifle, and the slug chipped brick from the corner of the bank building. Mulvane kept going up the alley.

He had his gun out now as he ran through the rain, and when he reached the far end of the alley he stopped and waited, wondering if anyone would follow him down here.

The sky was a leaden-gray, and even though it was not much past high noon it seemed almost like dusk, the shadows closing in around them. Mulvane waited at the far end of the alley, and then he saw a man running down the alley, a tall man without a slicker, a man with a black hat and black coat.

Rudabaugh was coming down this alley, and probably Bryant and the others were swinging down parallel alleys to come upon him from the rear. Rudabaugh had wanted his fight, and now he was going to get it.

Mulvane stepped out into the open, facing Rudabaugh squarely as the tall, lean gunman came down at a run. Rudabaugh was less than fifty feet away as Mulvane waited calmly, his gun back in the holster.

Seeing Mulvane in the alley, Rudabaugh pulled up abruptly, his white face ghostly in the murky light. Mulvane said, "Here it is, Rudabaugh."

Rudabaugh's luck this time was worse than it had been the first time. Possibly, because he'd been running he was still ruffled and out of breath; possibly, the rain had had something to do with it, and very possibly his luck had simply run out at long last.

Mulvane shot Rudabaugh before his gun was even out of the holster, the bullet doubling the thin man up, and he sank to his knees in the mud of the alley. He lifted his head once to look at Mulvane, and then he shook his head as if in disgust and toppled over.

Gun in hand, Mulvane raced up the alley, running past him and back again to the main street. He paused to look out, and he saw Ruby Watkins, Hannah Carrington, and the hotel clerk standing out on the porch of the hotel, looking in his direction.

Bryant, Bagley, and then men with Bryant had gone down the side streets to head him off, but anticipating that he would be coming out the same way he'd gone into the alley.

He ran across the road in full view of Ruby and the others, darting down another alley on that side, and then he swung right coming up on the rear of the hotel stables.

He paused here, breathing hard, and then he opened a rear door, seeing the old hostler just heading out toward the street. The old man had heard the shots and was going out to see who had been killed.

Mulvane stepped into the kitchen of the hotel. Finding it empty, he crossed rapidly to the dining room, and then into the empty lobby. As he crossed the lobby he could see the two women out on the porch, looking down the street, and as he watched he saw Bryant emerge from an alley and look up toward the hotel.

Hannah stepped out to the edge of the porch and pointed to the alley down which Mulvane had gone. Bryant disappeared, followed by his two riders.

Mulvane went up the steps to the second floor of the hotel, and then hurried to his room and stepped inside. The last place in this town where Ward Bryant would anticipate finding him would be in his room.

Locking the door behind him, Mulvane stepped over to the window and looked out around the drawn shade. He could see Bagley coming out of another alley and crossing the street, and he was a little surprised that Bagley was in this fight.

Mulvane pulled a chair up to the window and sat down, dropping his wet hat on the floor beside him. He rolled a cigarette and smoked it as he watched the window.

In about ten minutes he saw Bryant come out into the open again, heading down the street in the direction of the railroad station. One of the Rocking Chair riders was with him, and Mulvane was quite sure that the other man had now teamed up with Bagley.

Thinking about Rudabaugh now, he was surprised how easy it had been. He wondered ironically, if after outshooting a man like Rudabaugh, he was to die under the gun of someone like Ed Bagley. Life was full of surprises like that.

He sat for nearly an hour, watching the rain, occasionally catching glimpses of Bryant or Bagley as they searched every corner of this town. He wondered if they would eventually think of coming up to this room.

Once he heard a man moving down the hall outside his room, and he waited, listening, gun in hand, and then he heard a door open and close, and he realized that it was just another guest at the hotel.

The rain stopped after awhile, but heavy clouds were still sweeping across the town, and the wind seemed to have increased.

The coroner's wagon, evidently summoned by Bagley, had driven to the mouth of the alley, and two men carried the body of Rudabaugh out to the wagon, and then the wagon rolled off. Mulvane watched it go, thinking that it could have been himself inside.

At about two o'clock in the afternoon he saw the four men assembled together in front of Bagley's office. They were evidently arguing over some point, and Bagley seemed quite emphatic about it. Mulvane surmised that they were debating as to whether or not he'd skipped town, picking up a horse somewhere. They'd checked on his own claybank, finding the animal in the stable, but he could have gotten a horse almost anywhere, and ridden off in the rain.

As they talked, Hannah Carrington joined them, wearing a heavy, gray raincape. Soon she left, and Mulvane saw her, moments later, riding by in her buckboard, heading out toward Box C.

He watched her go, knowing that it was the last he would see of this woman whose ambition had destroyed her.

He surmised that she might be sending back a few of her riders to help Bryant in this manhunt, and it meant that he, Mulvane, could not wait too long now.

Leaving the window, he stepped to the doorway, unlocking it gently, and then moved out into the hall. He went down the stairs into the lobby, and as he crossed to the front door, the hotel clerk stared at him in amazement.

Mulvane looked out through the window, seeing Bagley and a Rocking Chair rider going by on the other side of the street. Bryant and the second man were heading in the opposite direction.

Then he heard Ruby Watkins' low cry of joy as she ran toward him from the dining room.

"Mr. Mulvane!" she whispered. "Are you all right?"

"Still alive," he smiled. "I'm obliged to you for getting me out of here."

"She's a wicked woman," Ruby said tensely, referring to Hannah. "I think she would have shot you. You've got to leave here, Mr. Mulvane!"

"More shooting to do," Mulvane told her grimly, and then he opened the door and stepped out into the street.

He followed Bagley and the Rocking Chair

man, keeping behind them, and walking on the opposite side of the street. Once he looked back to be sure Bryant hadn't seen him come out, but Bryant was still going in the opposite direction, unaware that Mulvane was on the street.

Mulvane walked a little faster, coming almost abreast of Bagley, and then the man with Bagley turned down an alley, and Bagley waited at the mouth of the alley.

Stepping out to the edge of the boardwalk, then, Mulvane called softly, "This way, Bagley."

Bagley spun around as if he'd been jabbed with a hatpin. He had his gun in his hand as he swung around, and the fear was in his face as he saw Mulvane across the street.

He brought up the gun hurriedly, and managed to get off a shot which was very wild, and Mulvane, remembering that this man had been in with Bryant right from the beginning, and had hired Rudabaugh to come here and kill him, put two shots into him calmly and coolly.

The man with Bagley whirled around, hearing the shots, and came running out of the alley, gun in hand, and as he did so, Mulvane dropped him with a bullet through the right shoulder. He fell, clutching at the shoulder, and Mulvane crossed the street hurriedly to pick up the gun he'd dropped.

Bagley lay in a loose heap in the mud, unmoving, sprawled on his face. He looked like a ragdoll which had been thrown out from an upper window.

Mulvane stepped out into the road and waited now. Ward Bryant had heard the shots, and was now running toward him passing the front of the hotel, his rider coming on behind him.

When Bryant saw Mulvane come out into the road, however, he slowed down. They were still forty yards apart when Bryant opened fire, moving toward him steadily as he did so.

The distance was quite long for a pistol, and Bryant's first two shots went wild. The third, however, tore through Mulvane's leather jacket, and he could feel the burn of it as it grazed his ribs.

He fired once, then, and Bryant stumbled as if he'd stubbed his toe against an invisible stone in the road. He still came on, though, the gun in his hand, but his head was hanging, and he was weaving as he moved in.

When he fired this time his bullet went into the mud. Mulvane let him go, turning his attention to the second man who'd leaped for the protection of the nearest building.

Mulvane's bullet, however, cut him down as he was leaping up on the walk, and he fell, his legs jerking as he went down.

Bryant was still coming on, stumbling, weaving, unseeing. His gun was empty now, but he was still squeezing on the trigger as he advanced.

When he was within ten feet of Mulvane he stopped, looking straight at his man, and not seeing him. Mulvane knew, then, that it was over. Bryant's knees gave way first, and he crumpled to the ground in a sitting position. Then very slowly his body bent over to the ground, and he lay there in the mud, less than six feet away from Ed Bagley.

Mulvane walked over to have a look at him, and then he holstered his gun and walked in the direction of the hotel.

Ruby had come out, and she was running down the walk toward him, her face white and strained. Mulvane caught her as she came up, and he had to support her with his arm.

"All over," he said. "All over."

She was leaning on his arm as they walked back to the hotel, and she said in a small voice, as if she had been considering this matter, and realized now that that was the way it had to be, "You'll be leaving now, Mr. Mulvane."

"I'll be leaving," Mulvane nodded.

They stood on the porch for a moment before going inside, and he looked toward the distant hills, black clouds hanging low over them. Beyond those hills was another place, another job. That place was calling him, and the call was stronger than Ruby Watkins. She knew it, and he knew it. She would find another young man in this town who would be willing to cut off his right arm if this girl would live with him on a little cattle spread.

Those hills were calling, though, and he had to heed the call. He could never be happy otherwise. Some day, somewhere, someone would knock him down, but that could be a long way off, and he'd never made a habit of worrying about tomorrow or the day after that.

"I'll see you before I leave in the morning," Mulvane said, "and I wish you much happiness, Ruby. You deserve it."

"Before you leave tomorrow," Ruby said. "I should like to know one thing."

He saw the sadness in her eyes, but in a girl so young that sadness would not last. She had high spirits; she had ambition; she had looks. This girl would not end up marrying some weak-kneed sodbuster and working herself to death before she was thirty-five. She would be married to a strong man, and she would manage her life wisely and well.

"What is it you want to know?" he smiled.

"You've never told me your name," she said.

"Mulvane."

"All of it."

Mulvane grinned. "Dad had a funny thing about names," he said. "When my older brother was born we were living near the Union Pacific tracks, so Dad named him Ulysses Patrocles, after the new railroad."

"Ulysses Patrocles!" Ruby said, laughing. "Why not Union Pacific?"

"Guess Dad thought a name like that would sound funny," he said.

"I see," she said. "But I still don't know your name."

He leaned over to whisper in her ear.

"Oh, my!" she said. Then she laughed. "It's kind of pretty, though."

She took his arm. "Come on, Mulvane," she said. "Take me in off the street, so I can say goodby to you properly."

They walked back into the hotel lobby together.

Center Point Large Print
600 Brooks Road / PO Box 1
Thorndike, ME 04986-0001 USA

(207) 568-3717

US & Canada:
1 800 929-9108
www.centerpointlargeprint.com